GHOSTLY TRICKS

A Harper Harlow Mystery Book Eight

LILY HARPER HART

HarperHart Publications

ONE

"Knock it off."

"You knock it off."

"I told you to knock it off first."

"And yet I'm the boss so that means you have to listen to me."

Harper Harlow narrowed her blue eyes and planted her hands on her hips as she glared at her best friend and roommate Zander Pritchett. He was in a mood – heck, they were both in moods – but she had little patience to deal with his fussy personality. "You're the boss?"

Zander, his dark hair gleaming thanks to some flattering lighting from the sun, nodded without hesitation. "Don't even bother arguing with the assessment. We both know I've been the boss since we met in kindergarten. You agreed to it back then so you can't back out now."

Harper made a face as she swiveled, fixing her boyfriend Jared Monroe with a pleading look. "Do you want to chime in here?"

Jared, who sat in a chair on the front porch and read the front section of the newspaper while drinking coffee, merely shrugged. He was used to listening to Harper and Zander argue. He knew better than inserting himself between them. The moment he did, the exact second he took Harper's side and told Zander to stuff it like she pretended she wanted, she would suddenly switch gears and take

Zander's side so Jared couldn't pick on him. There was no way Jared was falling into that trap again.

"I'm good," Jared supplied, never moving his eyes from the article he read. "It's starting to get chilly out here in the mornings, though. I just noticed it."

Shawn Donovan, Zander's boyfriend, snorted as he flipped through the sports section. Ever since Zander brought Shawn home – and didn't dump him, which was practically unheard of in the Harlow-Pritchett house – Shawn and Jared had formed a bond. They were the long-suffering love partners of two fiery and petulant individuals. They figured the only way to survive was to keep their heads down ... and join together in a united front ... so that's what they did.

"I heard that noise." Zander narrowed his eyes as he regarded his boyfriend. "Do you have something you want to add to this conversation?"

"Absolutely not." Shawn rolled his neck as he focused on the article in front of him. "How bad do you think the Tigers are going to be now that they're in rebuilding mode? I'm guessing it's going to be another long drought."

"I'm guessing you're right." Jared adopted an easy tone. "We never did get to a baseball game this summer, Heart. We should try to go to one next year. When I moved to this side of the state, I told my mother I would be at games all the time. I guess I was wrong."

Harper wrinkled her nose. "Is that somehow my fault?"

Jared flicked his eyes to her for the first time in at least ten minutes. "Yes."

"How?"

"Well, I had no interest in getting involved with anyone when I first moved here because I thought it was going to be a stepping stone to moving somewhere else," Jared replied reasonably. "Then I met you and lost my heart."

Harper's cheeks flushed with color at the romantic words. "That was kind of sweet."

Jared winked. "Losing my heart to you often makes me feel as if I'm losing my head," he continued. "Because I'm often so busy chasing you around – and trying to keep Zander from climbing into bed with us every morning – I didn't attend any Tigers games this season."

Harper's smile slipped. "That was less sweet."

Jared shrugged. "It comes and goes."

"I don't try climbing in bed with you every morning," Zander argued, offended. "You're exaggerating."

"I woke up this morning and you were gone," Shawn pointed out. "When I decided to find you, all I had to do was follow the voices. You and Harper were excitedly flipping through a Grandin Road catalog while poor Jared had a pillow pressed to his head to drown out the noise."

"That was one morning," Zander protested.

"That's almost every morning but the weekend ones," Jared countered. "Ever since I put my foot down on the weekend mornings you two have paid me back by doing it practically every weekday morning. It's starting to get obtrusive."

Harper tilted her head to the side, considering. "I guess I didn't think about that. It's uncomfortable for you, isn't it?"

"It's uncomfortable because he's worried he'll get hot for me," Zander muttered under his breath.

"See, I'm not going to rise to that ... er, so to speak," Jared said, glaring at Zander. "You want me to get worked up and deny it so you can whisper to Harper that I'm uncomfortable with my sexuality. I know how your mind works."

"Oh, well, la-di-da."

Shawn flicked Zander's elbow to quiet him. "Why do you have to pick a fight? We were having a perfectly pleasant morning until you jumped all over him."

Zander's eyes lit with anger. "I jumped all over him? That's freaking rich. That's not what happened at all."

"That's exactly what happened," Harper interjected, her worried eyes on Jared. She loved her boyfriend and best friend to excess, but Jared was chafing of late under Zander's insistence that he not only always be right but also to be the center of attention. "We need to come up with some rules."

"We already have rules," Zander complained. "And they're excessive. They're unneeded ... irritating ... and freakily excessive."

Harper kept her eyes on Jared as she discarded Zander's complaints. "Then we need to enforce them."

As if sensing her gaze, Jared lifted his eyes and smiled. "Heart, I don't want to start an argument."

"Oh, well, it's too late for that." Zander rolled his eyes, balking when Shawn scorched him with a dark look. "What? I'm completely innocent in this. Jared is the one who turned it into a thing."

"No, you're the one who turned it into a thing," Shawn said. "You're good when you set your mind to something, but I know how you operate, and constantly making Jared out to be the bad guy is getting old."

Zander's mouth dropped open in mock outrage. "That's not what I've been doing."

"That's exactly what you've been doing," Shawn countered. "Jared can't always be the one compromising. You need to give a little, too."

"I don't see why I have to give," Zander sniffed, folding his arms over his chest and adopting a far-off expression. "This is my house."

"It's my house, too," Harper pointed out. "Jared should feel welcome here. If he doesn't ... ." She broke off, chewing on her bottom lip as she internally debated some problem only she could see.

"I didn't mean to start a thing," Jared said, folding the newspaper and setting it on the table next to him. "I was merely joking with you guys. We don't have to start a fight."

He said the words, but Harper recognized the weariness behind them. He was tired and needed a break. The thing he needed a break from the most was Zander.

"How about we spend the night at your place after your shift, huh?" Harper suggested, hoping she came across as flexible and happy rather than deranged when she forced a smile.

Jared stared at her for a long beat, as if trying to read her mind. Finally, he shook his head and rubbed his hand over the top of his dark hair. "No, I don't think that's a good idea."

Harper's heart fell. "You don't?"

"No."

"Why not?" Zander was instantly on the offensive. "Is something going on here? Are you hiding something at your place? I know, he's probably got another girl there." He slapped Harper's shoulder for emphasis. "He clearly doesn't want you to see something, Harp. I knew this would happen from the start."

Jared pinched the bridge of his nose to ward off what he was sure would turn into a raging headache. "Really? You think I have a girl hidden at my rental, huh? How does that work? I spend every single night with Harper. You would think the other girl would catch on."

"She might not be very bright," Zander said. "She might think you're a superhero or something and you're out fighting crime and that's why you're gone every night. She probably even thinks you have a costume ... and super villain enemies loitering around Whisper Cove ... and a kicky little sidekick who just happens to run a gym." Zander's gaze was heavy when it landed on a snickering Shawn, who happened to be a gym owner.

"Wow. You've put some thought into this," Jared said dryly.

"Way too much," Shawn agreed.

"He's right, though," Harper offered. "You're definitely a superhero."

Jared read the worry on her face and snagged her around the waist, dragging her to his lap so he could kiss the tender spot behind her ear and snuggle against her. "Don't get worked up. I swear I don't have a girlfriend at the rental. Heck, I can barely remember what the rental looks like because I spend so much time here."

Harper cast him a dubious look. "That's why I suggested going there. If you're sick of Zander ... ."

"Hey!" Zander was annoyed. "No one is sick of Zander. Everyone loves Zander. In fact ... that should be a television show or something."

"Yes, and we'd all love to watch it." Shawn shot Zander a quelling look. "Be quiet and let Jared and Harper talk for a minute."

Zander's mouth fell open. "I have no problem with them talking. In fact, I'm happy to let them talk. I am not the type of person who tries to stop others from talking."

"No, that simply seems to be a byproduct of your exuberant personality," Shawn said. "Now ... shh." He pressed his finger to his lips to prod Zander to silence.

"Oh, well, this is simply ridiculous." Zander pressed his lips together and turned his eyes to the ceiling. "I'm being persecuted ... and probably for a reality television show. There can be no other explanation."

Jared ignored Zander's outburst – he was used to those, too – and slipped a strand of Harper's honey-colored hair behind her ear. The first thought he had the day he met her was that he'd never met anyone as beautiful as her in the real world. He still thought that, and even though Zander was often a royal pain in the butt, he knew he was lucky to have found love with Harper.

"I don't want to spend the evening at my place tonight for several reasons," Jared started. "The first is that almost every item of clothing I own is here. That would mean packing to go back ... and that's boring."

"Oh." Harper hadn't considered that, although it made sense. "Still ... we haven't had much alone time lately. You must be itching to be away from Zander for a few hours."

"Oh, you're jumping on the 'Smack Zander as if he's the school loser' express train, too, huh?" Zander was furious. "We're going to talk about this later, Harp."

Harper ignored him and focused on Jared. "I want to spend alone time with you, too. It's been a busy week and I lost track of time. I'm sorry about that."

"You lost track of time because you guys have been decorating for Halloween," Jared noted. "I had no idea you two were such Halloween fanatics, but it actually makes sense given what you do for a living."

In addition to being best friends and roommates, Zander and Harper were also co-owners of Ghost Hunters, Inc. – GHI, to those in the know – which meant they hunted for displaced spirits for a living. Since Harper could see and talk to ghosts, she provided the muscle. Zander had a business mind – at least most of the time – and he ran everything else. That meant they spent an obscene amount of time together between work and play. Jared was not only used to it but also fine with it ... other than the excessive morning visits from Zander, that is. He was completely over them.

"I do love Halloween," Harper admitted, resting her head against Jared's shoulder as she cuddled closer. "It's my favorite time of year."

"I figured that out when you asked me if I wanted to rake leaves and roll in them with you the other day," Jared teased.

"Ugh." Zander made a disgusted face. "You're supposed to do that with me."

"I was going to roll with him a different way than I roll with you," Harper shot back.

"Let's hope so," Shawn said. "Still, I think it's cute that you guys get so involved in Halloween. I love this time of year, too."

"It's my favorite," Harper admitted. "I love pumpkin-flavored everything. I love pumpkin-scented everything. I love candy ... and costumes ... and horror movies."

"See, I would've thought you see enough horror at work sometimes that you'd want a break from it," Jared teased. "I guess I was wrong, huh?"

"You were. We go all out for Halloween. We watch horror movies all month and you wouldn't believe the decorations we're going to start dragging down from the attic tonight. I mean ... that is if you don't want to head to your house to spend the night."

Jared considered messing with her but ultimately didn't have the heart to do it. "I don't want to infringe on the decorating. In fact, I find the decorating ridiculously entertaining. I don't want to spend the night at my house because it doesn't feel like home."

Harper didn't bother to hide her surprise. "It doesn't?"

"Nope. You feel like home, and you're more comfortable here."

"Oh, now I definitely want to spend some alone time with you." Harper smacked a kiss against Jared's cheek. "How about we get takeout tonight and lock ourselves in my bedroom to watch a horror movie? That will be like spending the night alone someplace else."

"I can live with that." Jared stroked his hand down the back of her head to smooth her hair. "For the record, I'm fine spending nights here. I'm fine hanging out here. I even find Zander tolerable most of the time."

"I heard that," Zander grumbled.

"I wasn't whispering," Jared shot back. "It's only the constant morning wake-up calls that drive me insane. If they're the least of my worries, though, I think I have it good."

"I know you have it good," Zander shot back. "Harper is like the best girlfriend ever. You should thank your lucky stars that she even lets you see her naked."

"And here we go." Jared heaved out a sigh and cracked his neck.

Harper recognized the annoyance before Zander could even open his mouth. "No, he's done." She shot Zander a dark look, the message clear. She recognized that Jared was doing his very best to keep his cool, but he was obviously close to losing it. Unfortunately, Zander recognized it, too, and he was keen to see how far he could push Jared. Harper had no intention of giving him the chance.

"No, he's done," Harper said, holding up a hand to quiet Zander before he could get a full head of steam. "He's just messing around. He can't seem to help himself."

"I figured that out the day I met him." Jared rubbed his thumb against Harper's soft skin, an attack of whimsy threatening to overtake him. "That was almost six months ago. It kind of feels like a lifetime ago."

"Because you're tired?" Harper asked.

"Because things have changed so much." Jared kissed the tip of her nose. "I mean that in a good way, too, so don't let Zander convince you I meant it in a negative way while I'm at work."

"Speaking of work ... ." Harper spared a glance for her phone screen. "Don't you have to get going?"

Jared worked as a detective with the Whisper Cove Police Department and his shift started in five minutes. Thankfully, the department was exactly two miles away so he had time.

"I do," Jared confirmed. "The good news is, things have been quiet for the past few weeks. No one has died and nothing out of the ordinary has happened. I'm hoping that streak will continue."

"Oh, well, it's not going to happen now," Zander noted. "You just jinxed yourself. Bad luck is coming your way, my friend."

"I think I've had my fill of bad luck." Jared pressed a firm kiss to Harper's mouth. "I will call you when it's close to the end of my shift and we'll decide on food. I'll bring it back ... and then you can tell me why you guys go so over-the-top with the decorations."

"We just like them."

"I guess it will be a short story then." Jared couldn't stop himself from sneaking another kiss before lifting Harper off his lap and moving down the front porch steps. "You guys be good and don't gang up on Zander because he's being a pain. He knows he's being a pain and he doesn't care."

"We're only going to do it because we love you," Harper called out, causing Jared to smirk.

"I love you, too. I'll be in touch."

Harper watched until he climbed into his truck, offering a flirty wave before turning her attention to Zander. Her smile disappeared when she caught sight of her best friend's smug expression. "We need to talk."

Zander scowled. "Yeah. I figured that was coming."

"You figured right."

2

TWO

"You're late."

Mel Kelsey, Jared's partner, barely looked up from the report he perused as Jared strode into the office area they shared. For his part, Jared merely shook his head.

"I'm like one minute late."

"That's still late."

"Since we're not exactly bursting at the seams with crime, I'm sure we'll survive." Jared poured himself a mug of coffee before sliding into his desk chair and booting up his computer. "I was having a discussion with your nephew and he wouldn't shut his mouth so I could leave."

In addition to being Jared's partner, Mel was also Zander's uncle. It made for some hilarious conversations at times, although Jared wasn't particularly thrilled with Zander at the moment so he wasn't feeling gregarious when it came to Mel's nephew.

Mel easily read the slope of Jared's shoulders and knew he was in for an earful. "What did he do now?"

"He didn't do anything different than he ever does," Jared replied. "He's just ... Zander."

"Yes, we've thought of having shirts made up that say that." Mel's tone was dry. He loved his nephew but understood that sharing a roof with him taxed a nerve or two. "What's wrong with him now?"

Jared sipped his coffee before speaking. "I don't know that anything is wrong with him. He's just ... in a mood. It seems he's always in a mood these days."

"So are you. I'm guessing that makes life difficult for Harper."

Jared had never considered that. "I don't want to make things harder for Harper," he hedged. "That's the last thing I want. He just wears on me."

"Give me an example."

"Okay, for example, this morning he climbed into bed with us and proceeded to spend an hour going through a Halloween catalog with Harper. They were loud."

Mel snorted. "Hey, I find the bed thing weird. You're not going to hear me arguing otherwise. I've always thought them sharing a bed was beyond the norm. It's hardly as if this is news, though."

"They're not sharing a bed," Jared clarified. "Harper and I share a bed. Zander simply insists on joining us five mornings out of every seven. It gets old ... and I kind of want to cut out his tongue some mornings."

Mel's expression turned serious. "Have you considered talking to Harper about it?"

"We have talked about it."

"And she refuses to do anything about it?"

"She ... ." Jared broke off, unsure how he wanted to respond.

"I don't blame you for being agitated," Mel prodded. "I wouldn't want another man in bed with me either. It has to be uncomfortable."

"It's not that. I like Zander. No, I really do. He's funny ... and loyal ... and he makes Harper laugh. I like him almost seventy-five percent of the time."

Mel snorted, genuinely amused. "He was also here before you."

"I'm not trying to supplant him. I don't want him gone. Harper would never be happy without him. It's just ... it's a lot to deal with. I wouldn't mind a bit of privacy."

"So, tell him that. Zander is reasonable."

Jared cocked a challenging eyebrow. "Since when?"

"Zander is reasonable if you explain things to him," Mel clarified. "He wants Harper happy, too. Don't get me wrong, the boy can be a righteous pain in the keister. That's what he does and he thrives on driving people insane. He doesn't want Harper upset, though. She's his Achilles heel."

"She's my Achilles heel, too," Jared pointed out. "I want a happy medium with Zander, but it seems that every few months he gets a bug up his butt and goes out of his way to irritate me. I can't figure out why he feels the need to do it."

"I don't think Zander knows why he does it. He's always been a persnickety thing. Even when he was a kid, he would have long stretches where he behaved himself and then out of nowhere he would fly off the rails and do something completely asinine. He gave his mother an ulcer here and there when he was younger."

"I don't doubt that for a second." Jared rolled his neck until it cracked. "The thing is, I thought things would get better when he started dating Shawn – and they did – but he still occasionally back-slides into irritation mode and I'm starting to find it less cute."

Mel narrowed his eyes as he regarded his partner. "I happen to like Shawn. I never thought Zander would find anyone to settle down with, but Shawn gives me hope. You don't think Zander is going to make a huge mistake and break up with him, do you?"

Jared immediately shook his head. "I think Zander and Shawn are fairly solid. Although, to be fair, I don't think Shawn likes the morning visits between Zander and Harper any more than I do. They're not happening in his bed, though, so it's not as hard for him to swallow."

"So what's the solution?" Mel was a pragmatic soul and he enjoyed fixing things. "How do you intend on adjusting Zander's attitude without turning him into a complaining mess?"

"That is the question." Jared held his hands palms out and shrugged. "I don't want to create a scene, but we need to do something. I don't know what – and I haven't decided how I'm going to handle things yet – but I'm in a tough spot.

"I know I don't want to lose Harper," he continued. "Part of me worries that if I push too hard that she might push back and the thought of that terrifies me."

Realization dawned on Mel's face. "You think she'll pick Zander over you."

"I don't want to think that," Jared corrected. "I'm not an insecure guy and I know Harper loves me. The thing is, she loves Zander, too. She's never going to abandon him. I don't want her to abandon him. We need some enforceable rules, though."

"I've known Harper since she was this high." Mel put his hand to his knee. "She's much more reasonable than my nephew. If you explain things to her exactly how you've explained them to me – don't start yelling or fall into histrionics or anything, mind you – she's going to see your side and help you come up with a solution."

"That's what I plan to do but we need some time alone for me to broach the subject. Right now, the four of us are essentially living under the same roof because Shawn is there every night, too. Alone time is almost nonexistent."

Mel made a sympathetic sound with his tongue. "I'm sure you'll figure something out."

Jared forced a tight-lipped smile. "That's the plan. For now, though, I don't want to talk about it. Let's focus on work. Do we have anything?"

"Just more pranks," Mel replied, turning to business. "I think it must be kids or something. Someone egged old Mrs. Bishop's house last night and toilet-papered that big tree in her front yard. She's spitting mad, but it's hardly a felony or anything."

"We've had a lot of pranks going down lately," Jared mused. "Is that normal for this time of year?"

Mel shrugged. "It's the run-up to Halloween. We get our fair share of pranks. You have to understand, it's Whisper Cove. We don't have a lot to do locally for the kids and if they don't want to drive for thirty minutes to hit a mall or Starbucks, they're forced to come up with their own form of entertainment."

"And that form of entertainment is vandalism?"

"Sometimes."

"Okay, well ... I guess we could run to the grocery store and see if they've noticed any specific kids stocking up on toilet paper, eggs, and shaving cream," Jared suggested. "Other than that, I have no idea what to do."

"That makes two of us."

"WE NEED TO TALK."

Harper and Zander spent two hours sorting through Halloween decoration boxes in the living room before she decided to address the obvious problem. Shawn left for work not long after Jared – he owned the local gym and worked long shifts on alternating days of the week – so the roommates had the house to themselves. Since they owned their own business and didn't currently have a client, they could essentially set their own schedules ... and that's exactly how they liked it.

"What do you want to talk about?" Zander was focused on a box of lights. "I don't remember using these last year. I think they would look cool wrapped around the front porch railing. They're purple and orange mixed together. That's a winning combination."

Harper spared a glance for the lights in question. "Those are for the kitchen. We ran them across the top of the cupboards last year. We used the lights that make it look as if it's thunder storming for the front porch."

Zander wagged his index finger. "Good call. I forgot about that. Do you remember where we left the tape?"

Harper bit the inside of her cheek to keep from exploding. Zander was purposely evading the "we need to talk" missive because he knew he was about to get in trouble. Harper had no intention of letting him slide off the hook. "Zander."

"What, Harp?" Zander adopted an innocent expression. "What did I do now?"

It took everything Harper had to hold back a dramatic sigh. That would only encourage Zander, and it was time for a serious discussion. "You need to give it a rest with the morning visits."

Zander pursed his lips. "I see. Jared laid down the law, huh? It's him or the highway. I'm the one out in the cold ... shivering until I die."

"Jared didn't say anything. He's not like that. He's trying to ignore the problem and approach me later, when he thinks there's a chance I won't take your side. He's worried I'll pick you in a fight and that causes fear. I don't think it's fair for Jared to live in fear."

"I'm fine with it." Zander was blasé as he held up an electric gazing globe. "Coffee table, right?"

Harper nodded but didn't avert her gaze. "No more morning visits for a bit, Zander. It's not fair to Jared."

"Yes, and everything we do has to revolve around Jared," Zander muttered, disgusted. "Do you remember when we could do things without having to clear them with Jared?"

Harper refused to be dragged into an argument. "It's not fair to Shawn either."

Zander balked. "Shawn doesn't complain about anything."

"Were you present for the same conversation as me this morning?" Harper challenged. "Shawn isn't a whiner so he couched his comments a bit, but he was hurt when he woke up this morning and you weren't in bed with him."

Zander stilled. "He didn't say that."

"He insinuated it."

"But ... ." Zander tilted his head to the side, considering. "Do you honestly think he was hurt? That's not what I was trying to do. He was asleep. I didn't want to wake him. I also had that catalog and you know how much I love Grandin Road."

"I do know that. We both love Grandin Road."

"So what's the problem with looking through a catalog?"

"There's no problem with looking through a catalog," Harper clarified. "We could've done it over the breakfast table, though. You can't keep climbing into bed with us. It makes Jared uncomfortable and I don't want that."

"Why?" Zander wasn't ready to back down. "A little discomfort never hurt anyone."

"Then why can't you be uncomfortable for a change?"

Whatever response he was expecting, that wasn't it. Zander made an exaggerated face that was so ridiculous Harper had to avert her gaze to keep from laughing.

"Why should I have to change?" Zander challenged. "This is my house."

"It's my house, too." Harper lowered her voice and adjusted her tone. "I love you. I'm positive you know that, right?"

Zander nodded. "I'm completely and totally lovable."

"You are. I love Jared, too, though. I don't want to lose him."

Instead of reacting with sympathy, like she expected, Zander barked out a laugh. "You're not going to lose him. He loves you as much you love him. In fact, he's totally whipped. He'll take whatever I can dish out."

Harper sobered, suspicion rolling through her. "Is that why you've been acting the way you have?"

Zander shrugged, noncommittal. "I have no idea what you're talking about."

Harper didn't believe that for a second. "You're not a very good actor. You'd better work on that. As for visiting us every morning, it's no longer allowed. In fact ... I'm going to start locking the door."

Zander let loose with a dramatic gasp. "You wouldn't dare."

"Oh, I would dare. It's going to happen. I mean it. Jared needs a break and you're going to give it to him."

"Well, that's just lovely," Zander snapped, hopping to his feet. "Basically you're saying that I have to follow Jared's rules in my house. How did that even happen?"

"Not Jared's rules, my rules."

"Oh, well ... ." Zander blew out a wet raspberry. "That's what I think of that." He turned on his heel and stormed toward the kitchen. "We need a timeout!"

"I was just thinking the same thing," Harper muttered, pushing herself to a standing position and grabbing the box of lights for the front porch. "I'll be outside."

"I would care if I were talking to you," Zander snapped from the other room.

Harper rolled her eyes and exited the house, resting the lights on the chair Jared sat in a few hours before. She shuffled to the railing and gripped it hard enough that her knuckles turned white, running through a bevy of mental exercises she'd perfected over the years when dealing with Zander's moods. She sucked in a series of deep breaths while letting her eyes wander to the beautiful foliage surrounding the house.

Whisper Cove was located close to Lake St. Clair in southeastern Michigan. The leaves didn't completely turn until halfway through October, but already the greens were mostly orange and yellow and Harper couldn't stop herself from marveling at the beautiful colors.

She managed a smile as she ruefully rubbed her forehead, tension building in her neck as she ran her conversation with Zander through her head. He was always difficult – most of the time because he enjoyed getting under people's skin – but he was being particularly obnoxious of late. She didn't like it.

Out of the corner of her eye, Harper caught a hint of movement and shifted her gaze to the neighbor's yard. The small house Harper and Zander shared was close to the river but had very little waterfront access. That was her only complaint about the house. Harper loved the river.

The house Henry Spencer owned, though, was another story. It looked almost exactly like the house Harper and Zander shared except it had a good eighty yards of waterfront property. Harper was jealous of the cantankerous old man's view.

Out of habit, Harper raised her hand and waved at Henry. He wasn't the friendly sort – often complaining that Harper and Zander were too loud when they hung out by the river – but he was older and lived alone so Harper felt the need to engage him in conversation when the opportunity arose. Henry wasn't within chatting distance – his hearing wasn't great – but he looked in Harper's direction and she was almost positive he frowned when he saw her. Instead of returning the wave, though, he merely stared.

Harper chewed on her bottom lip, something about the scene causing her heart rate to ratchet up. Something was wrong. She opened her mouth to call out to Henry, but the sound of the door opening behind her caused her to snap her head in that direction.

"I thought you might want to apologize," Zander sniffed, fixing her with a dark look. "I'm willing to listen if you're ready to talk."

Harper offered up a dismissive face. "I'm not sorry and you should be the one apologizing."

"Well, if that's the way you feel ... ."

Harper refused to let Zander's mouth run away with the conversation. "We have another problem."

"And what's that?" Zander narrowed his eyes. "Are you about to tell me what else I can do to make Jared happy in my house?"

"Maybe later, but that's not what I was talking about." Harper gestured toward Henry's house. "Do you see Henry on the front porch over there?"

Zander rolled his eyes but ultimately craned his neck to get a gander at the house. "No. He's probably inside."

Harper heaved out a weary sigh. "That's what I was afraid of."

"What?"

"I see him."

"You see him?" Zander looked again. "He's not there, Harp. The porch is empty. You can't be seeing him unless ... ." Zander broke off, realization dawning.

"Unless he's dead," Harper finished, resigned. "That's exactly what I think is going on."

"Oh, crud." Zander rubbed the back of his neck. "I suppose the old guy died in his sleep, huh? We should probably take a look. Or, wait, do you want to call Jared first and let him look? He is the important one, after all."

"I want to call Jared, but we have to confirm he's dead first," Harper said, refusing to rise to Zander's rather obvious bait. "We need to have a reason before we call. Otherwise he's going to have to make up an excuse on his report. We need to be sure."

"You are sure. You see Henry's ghost."

"Yes, but ... we need to see the body, too."

"Well, great." Zander threw his hands up in the air. "What a delightful way to spend our day. I'm so glad you suggested it."

Harper pursed her lips. "You'll come with me, right? I don't want to go alone even though I know he probably died of natural causes."

Zander nodded without hesitation. "I would never make you go alone."

"That's why you're a good friend."

Zander squeezed her shoulder. He was mad, but he could table it for later. "Does that mean we're done fighting?"

"For now."

"I'll take it."

THREE

"You just can't get enough of me, huh?"

Jared flashed a smile when he saw Harper pacing in front of her driveway. Her hair was a mess, her cheeks flushed with color, and she looked a bit crazy. Jared knew better than saying the last part out loud, though.

"Are you okay?" he hurried to Harper's side the minute Mel parked, tipping up her chin so he could stare into her eyes. "You seem ... upset."

Harper narrowed her eyes, suspicious. "You were going to say 'crazy,' weren't you?"

"Absolutely not."

Harper didn't believe that for a second. "He's dead."

"Henry?" Mel asked, moving to the front of the vehicle. "You're talking about Henry, right? That's what you said when you called."

Harper wrinkled her nose. "Who else would I be talking about?"

"I don't see Zander."

"Oh." Harper straightened her shoulders, something dark passing over her face. "Zander is fine ... for now."

Mel and Jared exchanged a look, something unsaid passing between them.

"I see." Mel ran his thumb over his bottom lip. "The thing is, I don't see him. Are you guys fighting?"

Harper adopted an airy tone. "Why would we possibly be fighting? That's ... ridiculous."

"Uh-oh." Jared slipped a strand of blond hair behind Harper's ear. "Did you guys get into it after I left?"

"We came to a meeting of the minds," Harper clarified.

"She was mean and told me I'm banned from her bedroom!" Zander bellowed, his face appearing on the other side of a window screen in the living room. "I don't like her right now ... especially after I selflessly went across the road with her and she told me I was being a baby when we caught sight of the body."

Jared pressed his lips together to keep from laughing. "I see."

"It's not funny," Zander groused. "I was here before you."

Jared sobered. "I ... ."

Harper cut off whatever her boyfriend was about to say with a firm shake of her head. "Don't engage him. He's in timeout!"

Jared pressed the heel of his hand to his forehead, confused and mildly amused. "I see. Well, why don't you tell me what happened and we'll figure out where to go from there."

"There's nothing to figure out." Harper's expression darkened. "He's going to respect the boundaries I set or he's going to cry when I wrestle him to the ground and ruin his new shirt."

Mel snorted. "Oh, geez."

"I was talking about with Henry, Heart," Jared said calmly. "If you want to talk about Zander, though, we can definitely do that. Later. We can't do it now."

"Of course you were talking about Henry." Harper felt like an idiot. "I knew that. It's just ... Zander makes me crazy."

"You make me crazy," Zander shot back. "I never thought you would be one of those women who tosses her best friend aside simply because she meets a pretty face but ... you have and it's done."

Jared fought the mad urge to laugh. Now was not the time to find amusement in their argument. "We'll talk about this later. We need to talk about Henry now."

"Your face isn't even that pretty!" Zander added.

Jared scowled, his calm demeanor finally breaking. "Don't make me come in there."

"Or me," Mel said. "You're being a baby. Come out of there."

"No."

"Fine." Mel wasn't in the mood to put up with his nephew's shenanigans. "Harper, we need you to tell us what happened with Henry. I know it's difficult because my nephew is a pain in the keister, but we're on the clock here."

"Right." Harper sobered, returning to the business at hand. "So, I came out to put some lights on the front porch and I saw Henry across the way."

"Was this before or after you and Zander started fighting?" Jared asked.

"After."

"Continue."

"There was something off about the way he reacted," Harper volunteered. "Usually he pretends he doesn't see us because he thinks Zander is loud – and possibly possessed by the Devil – and Henry pretty much hates us."

"He thinks you're loud, too," Zander barked. "Don't blame all this on me."

Jared rolled his eyes. "If you want to be part of the conversation, you need to leave the house and join us."

"I don't want to be part of your stupid conversation." Zander made a face. "I'm minding my own business in here and you're the ones trying to drag me into your conversation. Well, it's not going to work. I'm on to you."

Jared pressed the heel of his hand to his forehead, rubbing it to ward off an oncoming headache. "You make me tired."

"Get used to that," Mel said. "Go back to Henry, Harper. Did you see him fall down or something?"

Harper shook her head, turning serious. "Zander came out so we could argue some more and I had him look at Henry's front porch because I had a hunch. He couldn't see Henry, though."

"I don't understand." Mel's face was blank. "What does that matter?"

"It matters because Zander can't see ghosts," Jared supplied, resting his hand on Harper's shoulder. "Did you go over and check?"

Harper nodded, solemn. "I figured that was better for you. I didn't go inside or anything. It wasn't necessary. He's on the living room floor and ... he's dead. It's pretty obvious."

Mel's interest was officially piqued. "How can you be sure?"

"His eyes are open and he's staring at the ceiling. Oh, and his skin is blue."

"Oh, I'm sorry you had to see that." Jared gave Harper a quick hug, ignoring Mel's eye roll and Zander's derisive snort from inside the house. "You could've just called. You didn't need to check yourself."

"She's seen dead bodies before," Zander supplied, disdain practically dripping from his pouty mouth. "This is hardly the first dead body she's seen."

"I know that." Jared made a clucking sound with his tongue. "It's still not fair to her. Maybe if you were a better friend and went with her ... ."

"Hey!" Zander extended a warning finger. "I went with her. Just because we haven't made up, that doesn't mean I didn't go with her, you ... butthead."

Jared scowled. "Who are you calling a butthead?"

Mel cleared his throat to get everyone's attention. "We have a dead body, folks. Let's try to show some perspective."

Jared immediately turned serious. "You're right. I'm sorry. Letting our domestic disputes interfere with our work is uncalled for."

"Oh, don't get too down on yourself. Zander is a master at deranging people." Mel shot a challenging look in his nephew's direction. "He gets off on it."

"That is a dirty lie," Zander snapped.

"Whatever." Mel rolled his neck until it cracked. "We do need to get over there and check, though. If something really has happened to Henry ... well ... we need to handle it."

"Absolutely." Jared nodded before snagging gazes with Harper. "Are you going to be okay?"

Harper was surprised by the question. "I hate to state the obvious, but Zander is right. This is hardly the first dead body I've seen."

"I know but ... Henry was your neighbor."

"I don't think you understand," Harper hedged. "Henry was one of those 'hey, you kids, get off my lawn' guys." She shook a finger for emphasis and Jared was forced to swallow a smile. "He hated Zander and me with a fiery passion."

"He called me names," Zander added from inside the house. "He called me the Q-word ... and the F-word. Oh, and he used the D-word."

Jared could figure out the first two himself but the last one was a struggle. "The D-word?"

Zander let loose with a long-suffering sigh. "A dandy. He called me a dandy."

"Oh." Jared was back to being amused. "I'm sorry he did that."

"You and me both."

Harper merely shrugged when Jared's gaze returned to her. "He wasn't a nice guy. That doesn't mean I want him dead."

"No. I understand." Jared instinctively stroked his hand down the back of Harper's hand. "We'll go check."

"He's dead." Harper was firm. "Trust me."

"Well, we'll check anyway."

"Yes." Mel was anxious to put distance between himself and a warring Zander and Harper. "We'll check and then update you after that."

"We're looking forward to it," Zander said dryly. "It's wonderful to have Whisper Cove's finest ready to protect and serve at a moment's notice ... at least serve Harper, that is. If I were the one who needed help, on the other hand, you would let me die ... or cry ... or both."

Harper scorched him with a dark look. "Shut up, Zander."

"WELL, THEY'RE IN LOVELY MOODS," MEL NOTED AS HE walked up Henry's driveway with Jared at his side.

"I know. I'm worried." Jared's attention was back at Harper's house rather than focused on the dead body probably waiting for them.

"Why are you worried?"

"Because if I keep causing fights between Harper and Zander, eventually she's going to get sick of it."

Mel didn't bother to hide his eye roll. "You don't strike me as the insecure type, son. Why are you suddenly going that route?"

"They're best friends. I don't want to come between them."

Mel heaved out a sigh. The last thing he wanted was to position himself as an expert when it came to Zander – mostly because he believed Jared might abuse the privilege of his expertise – but he couldn't allow his partner to wallow. "They always fight like that."

Jared balked. "No, they don't."

"They do so." Mel wrinkled his forehead. "Sometimes I think you look at Harper with rose-colored glasses and believe she does no wrong."

Jared scowled. "I do not ... and she rarely does anything wrong."

"Yeah, I'm going to remind you of this conversation the next time you freak out because Harper took off on some wild ghost chase and you're furious and burning her name in effigy," Mel said dryly. "You're being ridiculous, though. Harper isn't going to choose Zander over you. Stop thinking like that."

"You don't know that won't happen."

"Yes, I do." Mel was at his wit's end. He hated feeling like the oldest man in the room, but that's exactly how Jared often made him feel. "Harper loves you. It's written all over her face whenever she sees you."

"Yeah, but ... ."

Mel refused to let Jared get a full head of steam. "She loves Zander, too, but she's hardly oblivious to his faults. He's a pain in the butt and she knows it. The thing is, Zander would never let things get to the point where anyone had to choose anything because he wouldn't hurt Harper that way.

"For a second, though, let's pretend Zander is evil rather than annoying," he continued. "Let's say he did try and force Harper's hand. Do you think she's so weak she would just sit back and let him dictate to her?"

"Well, no." Jared scratched at an invisible itch on the side of his cheek. "I can't help but worry. They're so connected that ... I can't help it. I don't know what to say."

"I think that you're a worrier by nature, son," Mel said. "It's not necessarily a bad thing, but it's a pointless thing in this situation. Harper is never going to let you go. I don't mean that in a creepy way, mind you. She's not going to turn into one of those women who locks a boyfriend in the basement if he breaks up with her or anything. Zander is merely feeling crabby right now and in need of attention. He doesn't want Harper upset, though. Trust me."

Jared heaved out a sigh. "I sound like a woman, don't I?"

"I think you're just trying to figure things out." Mel gave him a sympathetic pat on the shoulder. "You will. Don't worry. Until then, though, we should really check on Henry. Harper wasn't wrong about him being an old coot but that doesn't mean it's okay for him to be dead."

"Right." Jared forced himself to concentrate. "Let's do this."

"DO YOU THINK THEY'VE FOUND HIM YET?"

Zander was back outside, fake cobwebs in his hands as he worked on a window. He couldn't stop himself from occasionally glancing toward Henry's house.

Harper shrugged as she worked on the lights. "I'm sure they'll let us know when they have more information."

Zander slowly forced his eyes in her direction. "Are you still mad?"

"I'm not mad."

"You seem mad."

Harper heaved out a sigh. "I'm tired, Zander. It's already been a long day and it's not even lunch yet. I'm also ... worried."

Zander stilled. "Why? What are you worried about?"

"Jared. How long is he going to put up with this situation? I mean ... would you put up with us if you didn't have to?"

"I happen to think we're delightful."

"I think Jared probably believes that fifty percent of the time," Harper said. "The other fifty percent of the time, though, I'm going to guess that he finds us insufferable."

"Then he doesn't know how to have a good time."

Harper rolled her neck. "Can you please try to help me just a little bit?"

Zander was in no mood to capitulate and yet he couldn't hold out in the face of Harper's obvious misery. "I won't come in your bedroom while he's there."

"Really?" Harper was hopeful.

"That's what I said, isn't it?"

"I really appreciate it, Zander." Harper felt as if a weight had been lifted off her shoulders. "I know you don't like it but ... if things could calm down for a few weeks I'm sure they would get back to normal."

For the first time all morning, Zander fixed Harper with his full attention. "What do you mean by that? What's not normal?"

"I have this ... big ball of worry in my stomach," Harper admitted. "I don't know what it is or where it came from, but I'm afraid."

"Of losing Jared?" Zander discarded the remnants of his irritation and slipped into best friend mode. "Harp, Jared loves you. He's not going anywhere. If you believe that ... well, you're crazy."

Harper licked her lips. "I don't know what's wrong with me. I have this sense of dread following me around and I can't put a name to it. I feel like an idiot and yet ... well ... I simply can't shake it."

"Have you considered that Jared isn't the source of your dread?"

The question caught Harper off guard. "Not really."

Zander snorted. "I wouldn't admit that to him. He probably won't like it. Still, you're sensitive, Harp. If you're worried about something, if you're afraid of something, it might not be because of Jared. It might be because something else is going to happen."

Now Harper was completely confused. "If it's not because of him, why do I feel so sick to my stomach and afraid?"

Zander held his hands palms out and shrugged. "Maybe it has something to do with Henry. Maybe you realized something was going to happen to him before it did and simply didn't recognize what you were feeling."

Harper tilted her head to the side, considering. "I don't think it was that."

"Well, maybe it was something else paranormal," Zander suggested.

"I mean ... what you went through at the asylum was fairly terrifying. I know you didn't sleep for almost a week after we got back. Maybe that's still bugging you."

Harper averted her eyes. The trip to the asylum did still plague her, although she liked to think she was mostly over it. Being in close proximity to so many ghosts caused a sensory overload for almost two weeks. She slowly came back to reality after the trip, but the occasional nightmare still slipped in.

"I don't think it's that."

"You don't have to hide the fact that you were overwhelmed by what happened there." Zander lowered his voice. "We were all overwhelmed. That includes me and Jared, too. It's okay, though. We're both here for you."

"I know that." Harper chose her words carefully. "I don't think it's that. For the last week, though, I've been overwhelmed by fear. It's almost as if I'm being followed or something. I can't shake the feeling."

"And you think it's because of Jared?"

Harper shrugged, noncommittal. "Who else? I know I'll never lose you no matter how much we fight. The only other thing I love so much my heart might break is Jared. What else could it be?"

"Oh, well, a hundred different things." Zander tightened his grip on Harper's shoulders. "I think you're working yourself up for no reason. Harp, the odds of this ... feeling ... being because of Jared are slim.

"I'm not going to pretend he's my favorite person in the world right now, but he loves you," he continued. "I'm not talking easy and safe love. I'm talking 'grab you by the testicles and squeeze really hard' love."

Harper rolled her eyes. "Thanks for that visual."

Zander smirked. "The point is, he's not going anywhere. If you're inherently afraid of something, I don't think it's losing him. I think you're letting yourself get distracted by the idea it's him, but it's not him."

Harper wasn't convinced. "Then what is it?"

As if on cue, Jack Corgan's ghost picked that moment to pop into existence. He appeared in the spot next to the railing, causing Harper to take an inadvertent step back, and fixed the blond ghost hunter with a bland look.

"Imminent death and peril are on the horizon. We're all doomed."

Harper could do nothing but blink as she exhaled heavily. "I think I found my source of dread."

Corgan beamed. "Oh, that's the nicest thing anyone has said to me in years."

4

FOUR

One look in the window told Jared and Mel that Harper was right. It was obvious Henry was dead. They made entry through the open front door. It was unlocked, which made things easier, and Jared was grim as he knelt next to the older man's body.

"He's definitely dead."

"I'll call it in," Mel said, glancing around. "We need to think of something for the reports, by the way. Get your mind in gear."

Jared furrowed his brow. "What do you mean?"

"We can't really say that Harper saw a ghost. We need to come up with another reason for a welfare check."

"Oh." Realization dawned on Jared. "I didn't even think of that. Good idea."

"It doesn't have to be difficult." Mel let his gaze sweep over Henry's body. "There are no signs of foul play. I'm going to guess it was a heart attack or something else associated with natural causes. The medical examiner will tell us that, though."

"I guess we can just say that Harper stopped by to check on Henry because she hadn't seen him or something."

"I'm sure that will work. It's not as if we're going to question her on it and I can't see a reason why anyone else would want to poke holes in the story."

"I'll talk to her before we leave."

"I'm sure you'll kiss her, too." Even though they stood over death, Mel's eyes twinkled. "Don't worry. She's done this before. She'll understand."

"Right. Well, we should take a quick look around to be sure but there are no signs of violence here. I think you're right about natural causes."

"While you're looking around, I'll call Henry's daughter."

"Do you know her?"

"Carol Winstead. She's a lifetime Whisper Cove girl. She married a local boy about seventeen years ago and works as a secretary in Chesterfield Township. She's friendly, although an only child. Her mother died a few years ago I think. I'm sure this will hit her hard."

"Okay. You make notification and I'll conduct the search while we're waiting for the medical examiner."

"That sounds like a plan."

"WHAT ARE YOU DOING HERE?"

Harper made a face as she recovered.

For his part, Jack merely smiled and shrugged. "Can't an old friend stop in for a visit?"

As a former pirate – okay, he was a Great Lakes pirate so that's hardly Jack Sparrow territory – Jack was known for his roguish charm. He'd been wandering the area for a long time, and although Harper had only recently started talking to him, he was something of a local legend. Ironically, it was through Jack that Harper discovered her late grandfather also boasted the same ability she had. Supposedly, when she was small and hanging out with her grandfather, Jack stopped by for the occasional visit. She couldn't remember it but believed the craggy adventurer all the same.

"You don't often stop in for visits," Harper pointed out.

"Who are you talking to?" Zander asked, his eyes busy as they glanced around. "Is Henry's ghost here?"

"Not Henry. Jack."

"Oh." Zander's excitement faded. "I thought maybe Henry was going to stop by and tell us we were being loud and insufferable as a parting shot on his way out of town."

Harper shrugged. "He might yet. I know he's hanging around."

Jack's expression was unreadable. "What are you guys doing? Your house looks like it's haunted."

"That's the idea." Harper rubbed her sweaty palms over the seat of her pants. "Halloween is at the end of the month. We're decorating."

"Oh." Jack made a face. "You know, in my day, Halloween was an evil day. People locked themselves in their houses because they were afraid of the dark spirits. It wasn't something to be celebrated. Now all I see is Devil worshipers decorating. We're doomed, although I think I already told you that."

Harper had to bite back a laugh given the irony of the statement. "Really?" She cocked a dubious eyebrow. "Is that true or are you making it up?"

If Jack was offended, he didn't show it. "I don't make up stories to tell. The truth is far more interesting than fiction."

Harper didn't believe that for a second. "Well, Halloween is our favorite season. We love decorating for it and horror movies are a necessity in this house. We absolutely love getting dressed up on Halloween night and handing out candy to the kids."

"Right. I know something about that." Jack's face took on a far-off expression. "Your grandfather told me about it one year. He had the two of you with him at the time."

Even though she didn't want to encourage too many visits from Jack – it was obnoxious when he popped into her bedroom while she slept ... or changed her clothes – Harper was intrigued all the same. "We saw you on Halloween one year?"

"Is he talking about us?" Zander asked, returning to his cobweb work. "Ask him which Halloween it was. I'm curious."

Harper was, too. "How were we dressed?"

"Oh, well, I'm not sure." Jack mimed rubbing his chin. "I believe there was a tiara."

Harper snorted. "I never wore a tiara."

"Not you. Him." Jack jerked his thumb in Zander's direction. "He had some outfit on with really wide shoulders and tight pants."

"Oh, that must have been the year you dressed up as Prince Charming," Harper mused.

"Yes, and I'm still crushed you wouldn't dress up like Cinderella that year," Zander said. "You ruined the entire ensemble by dressing up as Princess Leia."

"Hey, you only said I had to be a princess. You didn't say I had to be a Disney princess."

"Yes, and I believe I was much more careful going forward when coordinating our costumes after that year," Zander said dryly. "Still, I did love that costume. Oh, and tell him it wasn't a tiara. It was a crown."

Harper wasn't sure that was true. She remembered Mel buying the "crown" for Zander and it came from the same bin they used when picking festival princess tiaras. Still, this was not the time for a second argument.

"I don't remember seeing you then, but it's kind of neat that you remember seeing us," Harper noted. "Did you go trick-or-treating with us?"

"I did for a bit," Jack confirmed. "Then I realized it consisted of begging for free goods and took my leave."

Harper pursed her lips. From Jack's point of view, that was probably an accurate description. "Oh, well ... fun."

"Yes, delightful." Jack rolled his eyes until they landed on Henry's house. "What is that vehicle?"

Harper followed his finger. "That's the medical examiner. He's here to collect a body."

Jack's eyebrows hopped. "Someone died?"

Harper nodded. "Our neighbor. He was old, though, so it was probably natural causes."

"Probably," Jack agreed, his tone pragmatic. "You can always ask the person who was sneaking around in the bushes last night if you need confirmation, though."

Harper stilled. "What?"

"Your neighbor got a visitor last night."

"You're sure it was last night?"

"I can keep track of time when I want," Jack replied. "I stopped by to see you, but you were busy making time with that other guy who lives here."

"Jared doesn't live here," Harper offered absently. "He just spends most of his nights here."

"Is there a difference?"

Harper ignored the question. "Did you see who was visiting?"

Jack shook his head. "It was dark and I didn't realize it was important to look."

"Could you at least tell if it was a man or woman?"

"Sorry but ... no. I was much more interested in watching you and your boyfriend."

Harper snapped back to reality, her expression indignant. "I don't think that's funny at all."

"Funny is definitely not the word I would use to describe what I saw," Jack agreed. "I had no idea you were so limber."

Harper smacked her hand against her forehead. "Oh, geez."

CAROL WINSTEAD WAS A SHAKING MESS WHEN SHE arrived at her late father's home. Since the medical examiner was working inside, Jared and Mel opted to interview her on the front porch.

"I'm so sorry for your loss," Mel offered, his expression sympathetic. "I hated making the call and I'm sorry you had to come out here under these circumstances."

"It's not your fault." Carol's hand trembled as she waved away the apology. "I'm simply glad you found him before ... well ... I'm glad he wasn't dead in there for days with no one looking."

"When is the last time you saw him?" Jared asked.

"Oh, well ... ." Carol screwed up her face in concentration. "I guess it was three days ago. I try to come here three times a week – even if it's only to stop in for ten minutes or so – and I was due to stop by after work today."

"How has his health been?"

"Honestly? I thought there was a chance he would outlive me," Carol replied. "He walked two miles a day even though he was in his seventies. His cholesterol was good. The doctor said he had the heart of a man twenty years younger."

Jared pursed his lips. "He didn't have any health issues?"

"No." Carol shook her head. "I was honestly surprised when I got the call. I wasn't expecting it."

"Well, the medical examiner is working inside now," Mel noted. "We probably won't have a cause of death for you until tomorrow."

"I understand." Carol forced a smile. "I just don't know what to think about this." She rubbed her forehead as she stared at the house. "He's never been the same since my mother died. I don't want to use the word 'depressed,' but I often worried about that. I tried to get him to move in with me so he wasn't always alone, but he wasn't keen on that."

"He liked his independence, huh?" Jared asked.

"Yeah. Plus, well, I have Marley."

"Who is Marley?"

"My daughter," Carol replied. "She's sixteen going on twenty-seven and she's a bit of a handful. She's hanging with a rougher crowd these days – you know, sarcastic, constantly shopping, and looking for places to party – and my father didn't like it. He was always chastising her even though I told him that was the exact opposite way to get a teenager to do what you want."

Jared offered up an encouraging smile. "I can imagine that having a teenager is difficult."

"It's not easy and Marley is kind of feeling out her boundaries right now. She doesn't mean to be difficult, but she does it quite well."

"That's a teenager thing," Mel supplied. "I remember when Zander was a teenager and I spent a good four years trying to figure out how I could tape his mouth shut."

Carol smiled, although the expression didn't make it all the way to her eyes. "That's right. Zander and Harper live right across the road."

Jared cleared his throat. "They're the ones who called us."

"They are?" Carol's eyebrows migrated higher on her forehead. "I wasn't under the impression that Harper and Zander were the sort to stop by. My father did nothing but complain about them, said it was unnatural for a man and woman to live together before getting married.

"I tried explaining that Zander was gay but that only made things worse," she continued. "He thought they were always up to something because they were running around and splashing in the river. He complained they were loud ... and way too touchy-feely."

"They are loud." Jared let loose with a kind smile. "It's okay. They're the first to tell you that they're loud."

"You date Harper, right?" Carol tightly pressed her lips together. "I forgot about that."

"I do," Jared confirmed. "She was upset when she called. She walked over because she said she usually sees your father outside and was worried. She looked in through the window and realized something happened so she called me."

"Well, tell her I'm glad she thought to check on him." Carol dragged a hand through her hair. "I don't even know where to start with all of this. When my mother died, my father made all of the arrangements."

"They have a list of things to do at the medical examiner's office," Mel supplied. "I'll have them email a copy to you."

"Thank you." Carol cast one more look at the house. "I don't think it feels real yet. I keep expecting him to come out onto the porch so he can complain about Harper and Zander's Halloween decorations. He did that every year – said they were garish – and I was gearing up for another round this year."

"We're very sorry for your loss." Jared was solemn. "If there's anything you need, don't hesitate to give us a call."

HARPER AND ZANDER WERE STILL ON THE FRONT PORCH when Mel and Jared swung by with an update.

"He's definitely dead," Mel said.

"We figured that out ourselves when the medical examiner showed up," Zander said dryly. "Do you know how he died?"

"There were no signs of a break-in or foul play," Mel replied. "We're assuming natural causes until we get the medical examiner's report. Although, to be fair, I don't expect anything dastardly to come out of their office."

"I wouldn't be so sure of that," Harper supplied.

Jared flicked his eyes to her. "Why do you say that?"

Harper shrugged, noncommittal.

Zander made a face as he rolled his eyes. "Because our friendly neighborhood pirate stopped by and he told Harper that he saw someone skulking around Henry's house last night. Now she's got it in her head that he was murdered."

Harper scorched Zander with a murderous look. "Thank you so much for sharing that."

Zander shrugged, unbothered. "Hey, it's the truth and I'm a truth teller. What more do you want from me?"

Harper muttered something intelligible under her breath as Jared studied her features. When she glanced up, she found him staring. "What?"

"I'm just debating whether you two are going to kill each other before the day is out," Jared replied. "I was hopeful you would make up."

Harper balked. "We have made up."

"You have?"

Harper nodded. "We hugged and everything."

"We did," Zander agreed. "The thing is, we often relapse when it comes to fight recovery. Don't worry about it. We'll be fine by the time you return for dinner."

"Oh, well, that's something to look forward to." Jared was blasé. "I don't suppose you want to give us more information about the person your ghost supposedly saw wandering around outside Henry's house last night, do you?"

Harper held her hands palms up. "I don't have anything to give you. Jack said he saw a shadow outside the house, but he was more focused on what we were doing."

Jared knit his eyebrows. "What were we doing?"

Harper shrugged. "I forget."

Zander snorted. "I believe Jack said you were doing something acrobatic."

Harper was mortified. "Who told you that?"

"You."

"Oh." Harper's cheeks flushed with color. "I forgot. Um ... we should talk about something else."

Jared looked as if the last thing he wanted was to let the conversation go, but he ultimately shook his head and wagged a finger. "We'll come back to that tonight."

Harper grimaced. "I can't wait."

"As for your ghost, Heart, just because he saw something, that doesn't mean that Henry was killed," Jared pointed out. "No one broke into that house. The door was open but not kicked in or anything. Nothing looked disturbed."

"Henry looked disturbed," Harper countered. "He was dead in the middle of his living room."

"Yes, and the television was on." Jared tugged on his waning patience. "Heart, it looks as if he was sitting in front of the television and had a medical emergency. He probably couldn't get to the phone in time and he died on the floor. Not everything is a murder mystery."

"I know that but ... ."

Jared shook his head. "I understand that your buddy Jack thought he saw something last night – that's when he wasn't distracted by what was going on with us, which we're still going to talk about – but the odds of Henry falling victim to foul play are pretty small right now."

"He was in his seventies, Harper," Mel added. "I know it's not what you want to hear, but sometimes a body simply gives out. That's clearly what happened to Henry."

Harper wasn't ready to give up. "What if it's not, though?"

"It is." Jared pressed a quick kiss to Harper's mouth. "Don't work yourself up, okay? Focus on your Halloween decorations. There's no reason to focus on Henry."

Harper considered arguing but instead plastered a watery smile on her face. "You're right. I just don't like thinking of him being alone over there when it happened."

Jared gave her hand a sympathetic squeeze. "I know. You have a huge heart. It's going to be okay, though. For once, this isn't a mystery you can solve."

"He's right, Harp," Zander said pragmatically. "You can't solve that mystery because it doesn't exist. You can solve this one, though."

Harper wrinkled her nose. "Which one?"

"The one where you favor Jared's needs over mine and lock me out of your bedroom."

Harper heaved out a rueful sigh. "Right. I should've seen that coming."

Jared grinned as he poked her side. "You really should have, Heart. I have to get going. By the way, if anyone asks, you went over there to check on Henry because you were worried, not because you saw a ghost."

Harper rolled her eyes. "I'm not new. I've got it."

"Good." Jared gave her another kiss. "We'll talk about the spying ghost when I get back."

Harper scowled. "I'm going to kill Zander ... or at least tape his mouth shut."

"If you figure out how to make that work, let me know," Mel said. "As for the other stuff, don't get involved. This isn't a mystery this time and I'd like to keep things simple."

Harper mock saluted. "Your wish is my command."

"That's not even remotely cute," Mel complained.

"No," Jared agreed, smiling. "It's flat-out adorable."

"Ugh. You two make me sick."

5

FIVE

"**W**hat's wrong with you?"

Mel cast his partner a sidelong look as they watched Henry's body being rolled out of the house on a gurney. Jared had been unnaturally quiet since leaving Harper and Zander, something Mel wasn't used to.

Jared shrugged, noncommittal. "I'm just thinking."

"You're thinking about what Harper said, aren't you?"

"I always think about what she says. She's smart."

"I never said she wasn't. I don't think she's right on this, though. Henry clearly died of natural causes."

"We don't know that," Jared hedged. "Just because it looks to be natural causes, that doesn't mean it is. It could be something else."

Mel fought the urge to roll his eyes. "Like what?"

"I don't know. Let's wait until the medical examiner gives us a ruling."

Mel snorted. "You're going to see that the medical examiner rules natural causes – whether a heart attack, stroke or something else – and then you're going to feel silly for dwelling on this."

"I hope that's true." Jared rubbed the back of his neck as he glanced around the house's interior. "On a different note, it's kind of weird how similar this place is to Harper's house. The colors are different and everything, but the house is exactly the same."

"I'm pretty sure they were built by the same developer." Mel was much happier talking about house construction than potential ghosts. "It was back in the early nineties. There used to be three ramshackle cottages on this lot, Zander's lot, and the one to the east. They built these in the nineties and they were a big deal, although Henry snapped up the one everyone wanted."

Jared was intrigued. "Because it has the best access to the river?"

"Exactly. Harper and Zander have access to the river, but they have to walk to get there. This house has a window that looks right out on the water and it's quite the view."

"It definitely is," Jared agreed, his eyes landing on the spot where Harper's hammock rested during the summer months. They spent many a summer day sharing the hammock, reading and talking, and he was sad to think he would be cut off from the activity until spring. "It's a nice house. I wonder what Carol is going to do with it."

Mel shrugged. "Maybe she'll move here. Her house is nice, but the view on this one is nicer. Of course, the house needs a little work because Henry didn't keep it up the way he should. Carol can hire someone for that, though."

"Yeah. Maybe." Jared shook himself out of a potentially dangerous reverie. "Do you think Harper and Zander will stay out of things given your warning?"

Mel let loose with a loud guffaw. "You act as if you just met them."

Jared considered the situation. "They're going to investigate anyway, aren't they?"

"As long as there's a chance Henry didn't die of natural causes, they're going to stick their noses in this investigation," Mel confirmed. "That's what they do. They can't seem to help themselves."

For some reason, the realization that Mel was right didn't bother Jared as much as it normally would. "Hopefully they'll be wasting their time on this one. Even if they spend a day poking around, if the medical examiner comes back with a natural causes death ruling, they'll have no choice but to let it go."

"You're cute." Mel made a big show of ruffling Jared's hair as if he were a small child. "You'll learn soon enough that Harper and Zander aren't about to be dissuaded by something like pesky facts."

Jared made a face. "Great. Now I have something else to worry about."

Mel smirked. "Get used to that. You picked a feisty woman. She's not going to stop being that way simply because you're around."

"I don't want her to stop being who she is." Jared was telling the truth. "If she would stop finding trouble so often, though, I would be fine with that."

"Here's hoping."

Jared nodded as he gave the house a final look before they locked it up. Here's hoping, indeed.

"DO YOU THINK HENRY DIED OF NATURAL CAUSES?"

Another two hours of house decorating made Zander and Harper realize they needed a treat to fuel them through the rest of the day. Since it was fall rather than winter, they opted for chili at the local diner instead of ice cream, their argument from before discarded in the wake of the body discovery.

"No." Harper saw no reason to lie as she sipped her Diet Coke. "I think he died for another reason."

"Do you think the medical examiner is going to agree with you?"

Harper shrugged, unsure. "I think that we need to track down Henry and find out what he has to say."

"And you're sure you saw his ghost this morning, right?"

"That's why I asked you to verify it." Harper knew she sounded irritated, but she couldn't help herself. "I saw him, Zander. He was there. How else do you think I knew he was dead?"

Zander held up his hands in mock surrender. "I wasn't calling your ability into question. That's not how I operate. You know I believe in you. Always."

Harper managed a rueful smile. "I know. I'm sorry. It's just ... did you see the look on Jared's face?"

"Oh, geez." Zander made a big show of rolling his eyes. "Are we back to talking about Jared?"

Harper ignored his tone. "He thinks I'm nuts."

"He doesn't think you're nuts. Uncle Mel thinks you're nuts. Jared thinks you walk on water."

Harper wrinkled her nose. "Do you have to always be so down on Jared? He's a good guy. I know he irritates you ... ."

Zander held up his hand to quiet Harper. "He does irritate me, but not for the reasons you think. I happen to like him ... er, well, at least for the most part. He's good to you. He dotes on you like you deserve. He's even funny when he's not messing with me."

Harper pursed her lips to keep from laughing at Zander's serious expression.

"By the way, I do think he's a good guy," Zander continued. "It's clear he loves you. I want you to be happy. If I played for the right team, I would like to think I'd be the one making you happy. Since that's impossible, he's a decent enough backup."

Harper's expression shifted to earnest. "I think that idea makes me uneasy. You're my best friend for a reason. If you want me to imagine us being together in a different way, well, I'm going to need a stiff drink ... or ten."

"Not to derail the conversation, but we should totally pick up some Godiva liquor on our way home and make chocolate martinis tonight. It's the season for chocolate overload, and we haven't had those since last winter."

Harper nodded without hesitation. "I'm open for that."

"Good." Zander returned to the conversation at hand. "As for Jared, I like him. I can't help myself if I like messing with him, though. And, yes, there are times I feel like I'm being pushed out by Jared. I know it's healthy and all that crap I'm supposed to say, but it still bothers me. I don't want you working yourself into a lather about it, though."

Harper made a face. "I hardly think I'm working myself into a lather."

Zander wasn't about to be distracted. "You're close. You need to admit it and move on. If you ask me, you're being ridiculous. I'm going to guess this is residual angst from our trip to the asylum, though, and hope you get over it before Halloween because otherwise you're going to ruin our favorite holiday."

Harper rolled her neck, agitation evident. "I'm not suffering from residual angst."

"I think you are." Zander refused to back down. "I love you, Harp. I always have and I always will. You're something of a fussy pain in the butt when you want to be, though.

"You think I don't get it, but I do," he continued. "You saw a lot of things there, things we couldn't see, and you're still grappling with some of the things that happened. No one wants to push you to get over it before you're ready."

Harper balked. "I am not freaking out over the trip to the asylum. I don't understand why you think that."

Zander ignored the argument. "It's okay. Jared understands. I think you're fixating on him, though, so you don't have to think about the rest of it. The problem with that is that you're making a mountain out of ... well ... nothing. Jared isn't going anywhere. It doesn't matter how much I irritate him."

"You don't know that," Harper argued. "He might get to the point where he says 'enough is enough' and walk out."

"No, he won't." Zander turned serious. "He's in it for the long haul. I see it whenever he looks at you. Why do you think I enjoy torturing him so much?"

"Because that's how you stay young."

Zander's grin was impish. "True, but I also do it because I know he's going to eventually take you completely away from me."

Harper immediately started shaking her head. "That's not going to happen."

"No, not in the way you're thinking," Zander agreed. "You will eventually get married, though. That means you'll move to a different house. Things are changing for us ... and while I'm excited I'm also a little nervous. I can't help it."

Harper opened her mouth to argue, a promise that she would never move on the tip of her tongue, but instinctively she knew she couldn't keep that promise. Eventually, if things went as she hoped, she would move. That didn't mean she would ever distance herself from Zander – some things were meant to be and her friendship with Zander was one of those things – but they couldn't be roommates forever. Harper wasn't a fool.

"I can see your mind working," Zander teased, wiping the corners of his mouth with a napkin. "Don't freak out. I've already made plans for your room when you move out."

Harper rolled her eyes. "Oh, yeah? What?"

"I'm going to turn it into an office."

"What if Shawn wants to do something else with it?" Harper teased. "Maybe he'll want to put mirrors on the wall so you guys can look at your reflections while lifting weights." Harper expected Zander to come up with a hasty excuse why that would never happen – mostly because he abhorred the idea of settling down – but he didn't.

"We might do that." Zander smiled. "We have plenty of time to talk about it down the line."

"I'm impressed," Harper said. "You didn't get a twitch in your eye or anything when you said that. I guess that means you really are looking toward the future rather than searching for an escape hatch."

Zander shrugged, his face unreadable. "I love Shawn."

Harper's mouth dropped open. She'd never heard Zander utter those words for anyone but herself. "Wow."

"We're going to be a happy foursome for a long time. Jared knows it. I know it. Shawn knows it. You're the one living with unnecessary doubt."

Harper dragged a hand through her hair. "I guess that means you think I'm being ridiculous."

"Always."

"I don't know what's wrong with me," Harper admitted. "I'm uneasy. I feel as if something is about to happen."

"It is about to happen," Zander said, inclining his chin toward the diner's front door. "Isn't that Marley Winstead?"

Harper glanced over her shoulder, furrowing her brow when her eyes fell on the pretty teenager, who also happened to be her dead neighbor's granddaughter. She wasn't alone, a tall boy in a letterman's jacket strolling behind her, and the duo looked deep in thought as they took the booth behind the one Harper and Zander shared.

"I can't believe this weather," Marley complained. "It's only October and it feels like December."

Harper narrowed her eyes as she listened. "She must not know," she whispered to Zander.

"I guess not." Zander stared at the boy with Marley. "I'm pretty sure that's Mike Dunlap with her."

Harper's face was blank. "Is that supposed to mean something to me?"

"He's the quarterback of the football team."

Harper wrinkled her forehead. "How can you possibly know that? It's not as if we hang out with high schoolers."

"No, but the football team spent the entire summer working out at Shawn's gym. I got to know them ... but only because they enjoy gossiping as much as me and they all think you're hot."

Harper was horrified. "Excuse me?"

"Oh, don't be a baby about it," Zander complained. "Teenage boys think you're hot. That's a good thing."

Harper felt dirty rather than elated. "I could be their ... older sister."

Zander snorted. "Yes, well, everyone loves a hot older sister." He dug in his wallet and came up with some cash, which he discarded on the table to pay the bill and cover the tip. "I was thinking we could head over to that big Halloween supercenter on the way home. It's only about twenty minutes out of our way. If this might be our last Halloween together, I think we should do it right."

Harper balked. "This is hardly our last Halloween together. No one is dying."

Zander rolled his eyes. "You know what I mean. Don't turn into a whiner."

Harper did her best to refrain from purposely tripping Zander as she stood, fixing Marley with a sympathetic smile as she made her way past the girl's booth. She knew better than breaking Henry's death to the girl and yet she couldn't stop herself all the same, something instinctual taking over.

"I'm sorry about your grandfather." The words were out of Harper's mouth before she could think better about uttering them. "I'm sure it's a terrible loss for you."

Instead of reacting how Harper expected, Marley merely shrugged. "He was old."

Harper's heart stuttered. She thought for sure Marley didn't know about her grandfather's death and she would be crushing the girl with the news. Apparently Marley did know ... and she simply didn't care. "But ... I thought he was in good health," Harper hedged. "I saw your mother talking to the police this morning and she looked upset. She seemed surprised by his death and shaken by the suddenness of it."

Marley's expression was blasé. "He was still old. I don't think his death surprised anyone. My mother is making a big show about it but that's what she does."

"Why were the police there?" Mike asked, drawing Harper's attention to him. "I thought he had a heart attack or something."

"He did," Marley said. "I don't know why the police were there either."

"The police are called whenever a body is discovered," Harper answered automatically, her mind busy. "It's standard procedure."

"See. She knows." Marley flipped open her menu. "I'm starving. I think I'm going to get soup and a sandwich."

"That sounds good to me, too," Mike said. "My stomach growled all the way through fifth and sixth periods."

Harper exchanged a quick look with Zander. She couldn't believe Marley's attitude. Zander looked as agitated about the situation as Harper felt.

"Well, I'm sorry for your loss," Zander said pointedly. "It's hard when you lose someone you love and even though you're putting on a brave face, I'm sure you really loved your grandfather."

Marley didn't adjust her attitude in the slightest. "He was a mean old man who told me I dressed like a harlot − although I had to look up that word to figure out if it was an insult − and acted like a crazed nutbag whenever he caught me hanging out with my friends. I didn't love him."

Harper's mouth dropped open at the girl's crass words. "But ... he was your grandfather."

Marley shrugged. "So what? You don't have to love someone simply because he or she is a relative. That's not the way the world works. Don't look at me like that. It's not as if he loved me either."

"I don't believe that."

"Why?" Marley refused to back down. "You knew him. You lived next door to him. All he did was complain about you guys. He thought Zander pretended to be gay so you guys could live in sin together. He told people that, even though I told him that didn't matter in this day and age."

Zander scratched an invisible itch on the side of his nose. "It's kind of like *Three's Company*. You know how I feel about *Three's Company*."

Harper refused to smile even though Zander's expression made her want to do just that. He really did love *Three's Company*. They watched it on weekends while bored. "Listen, Marley, I know your grandfather was difficult. He was still your grandfather." Harper opted to take a different tack. "I'm sure you're trying to be brave right now – and that's okay – but it's okay to cry over your grandfather. I happened to be really close with my grandfather when he died and it still makes me sad to think about it."

Marley's expression was so derisive it forced Harper to take an inadvertent step away from the table.

"I'm not going to change my mind," Marley said. "That man was mean and I'm not sorry he's gone. In fact, I'm kind of happy. He said he was going to leave me something good in his will. To me, that's the best part about all of this."

Harper was dumbfounded. "But ... ."

"Let it go, Harp," Zander instructed, making a tsking sound with his tongue as he shook his head and directed Harper toward the door. "It's a losing battle and she clearly doesn't care."

"Finally, someone who actually listens to what I say," Marley said. "I'm so excited. Can you talk to my mother and show her how it's done?"

Zander opted to ignore her. "Come on, Harp. Let's go to that Halloween store and do some shopping."

Harper had no idea what to say so she merely nodded. "Okay."

"That's my girl."

6

SIX

Jared found Shawn watching television when he let himself into Harper's house shortly after his shift ended. He took a moment to cock his head and listen, but it was obvious Zander and Harper weren't home.

"Where are the fearsome twosome?"

Shawn smirked. "They're at the Halloween supercenter buying more crap. They've been there for hours."

Jared arched an eyebrow. "Do they need more Halloween stuff?"

"They seem to think so."

"Well, it's their house." Jared shrugged out of his coat and hung it in the front closet. "Did they say when they would be back?"

"An hour ago."

Jared sat on the couch next to Shawn, his mind working. "That must mean they're buying a lot of stuff."

"I've learned that Zander doesn't do anything small. I don't think Halloween is going to be the exception. He's already trying to think up costumes for all four of us that tie in together."

"Oh, man." Jared rolled his neck and stared at the ceiling. "That doesn't sound like what I had in mind for Halloween."

"Harper likes Halloween as much as Zander. I don't think you're going to get out of wearing a costume."

"I don't mind a costume. I'm simply worried that Zander is going to pick costumes that make us look like idiots."

Shawn pursed his lips. "You don't know. He could pick something cool."

Jared wasn't convinced, but he knew better than launching into a diatribe about Zander's clothing choices. Shawn would stand up for Zander no matter what, which is the way it should be. Jared did the same for Harper so he understood.

"So, how was your day?" Shawn asked, changing the subject. "I heard the neighbor died and you got called out."

"It looks like natural causes, but we won't get the report from the medical examiner until tomorrow."

"I don't get the feeling that Harper believes it was natural causes." Shawn's eyes were serious when they snagged with Jared's. "Zander mentioned a ghost."

"That doesn't mean the death wasn't natural causes."

"I agree, but I'm not the ghost expert. I figure that's for you to explain to them when they get back."

"Yes, and I'm really looking forward to it," Jared drawled, eliciting a snicker from Shawn. "I'm actually kind of glad they're not home yet. That gives me a chance to talk to you about something that's been bothering me."

Shawn muted the television. "Is this about to turn bad?"

"I hope not. It's just ... where do you see things going in the next few months?"

The question caught Shawn off guard. "Between you and me? Um ... I thought we would continue to hang out with Zander and Harper. Did you have something else in mind? If so, I don't think Zander is going to like it. He already thinks you and I gang up on him at times when we attempt to rein in one of his ideas."

Jared made an exaggerated face. "Not that. Geez."

Shawn held up his hands. "I was simply asking."

"I'm talking about us as a foursome," Jared clarified. "I'm starting to feel as if this house isn't big enough for two growing relationships and the privacy needed for both of them to flourish."

"Oh." Realization dawned on Shawn. "Yeah. I've been giving that some thought, too."

"You have?" Jared was relieved. "I thought I was the only one feeling the pinch."

"You're not, but it's a sticky situation," Shawn pointed out. "They've lived together a long time. They're set in their ways. I've tried talking to Zander about hopping into bed with you guys, but he always brushes me off."

"That bothers you, too, huh?"

"It doesn't bother me to the extent it bothers you," Shawn replied. "I'm not worried about Zander being in bed with another guy or anything. I get that he's hanging with Harper. I would like to wake up with him more than two mornings a week, though. I honestly don't think he understands why you don't like being invaded and I'm not a fan of being abandoned."

"I never really thought about it that way." Jared rubbed his cheek. "It can't be any easier for you than it is for me, just for different reasons. I think we need to come up with a plan to move forward, but I'm honestly worried that Harper and Zander are going to fight any efforts to separate them."

Shawn was somber. "Do you want to separate them?"

"Not in the way you think. It's more that I want quiet time with Harper that doesn't involve Zander. They're best friends and I don't think either one of them would do well with limitations. That's not exactly what I'm getting at. Still, we can't all live together forever."

"Technically you and I have our own homes," Shawn reminded him. "Zander spends the night with me at my place occasionally, but those visits are getting fewer and far between. This is his home and it's where he's most comfortable."

"I like this place. It feels like home to me, too. The house I rent feels empty whenever I stop by. It's just ... I want a future with Harper. That means she's going to eventually have to move away from Zander."

"I want a future with Zander, too. I'm not sure he's ready to entertain separate households, though. I expect a huge meltdown when I broach the subject."

Jared leaned forward, intrigued. "And when do you think you might broach it?"

Shawn wagged a finger to dissuade Jared. "See, you're trying to put the onus of this on me. I don't think that's fair. You've been dating Harper longer than I've been dating Zander. You should be the one to bring it up."

"No, no, no." Jared vehemently shook his head. "If I do it, Zander will think I'm trying to steal Harper from him. If you do it, he'll think you're trying to keep him for yourself. There's a difference."

"You just made that up."

It was the truth, but Jared had no intention of admitting that. "I think it makes more sense for you to do it."

"And I think you want me to be the one to fall on a metaphorical sword, so to speak," Shawn argued. "You should talk to Harper and have her approach Zander. He'll be much more likely to listen if she's the one speaking."

"I don't know if that's true. They were in a big fight this afternoon."

"And yet they clearly got over it enough to shop."

Jared let loose with a long-suffering sigh as he rubbed his forehead and leaned back. "Zander is so much work. I think you must be a saint for putting up with him."

"It's not as if Harper is easygoing all of the time. She freaks out, too."

"Not as much as Zander."

"Well, Zander is an original." Shawn grinned. "We do need to figure out something, but I would be lying if I said I wasn't terrified to bring up the subject with Zander. He's hard to read. He could think it's a good idea or he could freak.

"There's also the fact that they own this house together," he continued. "One of them is going to have to sell to the other and find another house. That's a big undertaking and I don't think Zander is going to be open to moving. He loves this house and is the one who did the bulk of the decorating."

"Yeah. I've been thinking about that, too." Jared scratched his chin. "Harper loves the house, but I think she'll want to leave it for Zander because he hates change. If we're going to move, it's going to have to be close. Zander and Harper can't take being a great distance from one another."

"They're unbelievably co-dependent," Shawn agreed. "Do you have an idea?"

Jared shrugged. "Not yet, but I'm going to be giving it a lot of thought over the next few weeks. I want to look forward and here we're all stuck in really thick mud sometimes. I don't dislike having Zander around because he makes Harper happy, but we can't keep this up."

"So ... our plan is to come up with a plan?"

"Yup."

"Sold." Shawn grinned as he turned his attention to the opening front door, his eyes widening when Zander strode through the opening with his arms full of packages. "What did you guys buy?"

"They had some great stuff," Zander said. "The car is full. We're going to need your help to get everything inside."

Jared groaned. "You guys had plenty of stuff. Did you really need more?"

Zander fixed him with a hard look. "What do you think?"

Jared made up his mind on the spot. "I think I'm helping you carry stuff inside."

"Good boy."

"YOU GUYS ARE GOING TO BE DECORATING FOR DAYS," Jared lamented, eyeing the mountain of goods on the living room floor with overt disdain. "I can't believe you bought this much stuff. How much did you spend?"

Harper shrugged. "They had really good choices this year and we've always wanted to do an animated cemetery in the front yard. We never could before because Henry complained about the noise. That won't be an issue this year."

"Yes, well ... it's your money." Jared pressed a quick kiss to the corner of Harper's mouth. "I suppose you're going to want help putting all this stuff up."

"We're going to do it tomorrow," Zander interjected. "We've already taken the day off."

"It must be nice to own your own business," Jared said. "If I tried to take the day off to decorate I would be fired."

"We're between jobs," Harper reminded him. "Plus, Molly and Eric are spending a lot of time together and trying to figure out if they're in a relationship or merely a fling. In another week, I'm going to be loaded up with cemetery tour gigs. You're going to wish I was home putting up decorations because I'm going to be really busy ... and at night."

Jared handed Shawn a pizza menu, never moving his eyes from Harper. "You know, I think you mentioned something about that when we started dating. I can't really remember what you said, though."

"Harper does cemetery tours and tells ghost stories for groups all across the area during October," Zander supplied. "She's in high demand and we don't stick to local cemeteries. We go to Oakland County and even over to Ann Arbor at times. It's a big deal."

"Do you make a lot of money doing it?"

Harper nodded. "Do you know how retail stores say they make all their money before Christmas? That's kind of how it is for us. We make a ton of money in October. The only problem is, we work almost every day. It's a pain, but it makes the rest of the year easier."

"Well, while I won't like being away from you at night, I do like the idea of you conducting tours rather than chasing murderers," Jared noted. "That will put my mind at ease a bit."

"You know not all ghosts are friendly, right?" Zander challenged. "The ghosts hanging at some of these cemeteries are murderous jerks."

Jared's smile slipped. "Did you have to tell me that?"

"It will be fine," Harper said, lightly pushing Jared so he had no choice but to sit in the chair at the edge of the room. She climbed on his lap and gave him a firm kiss on the cheek. "In fact, if you're worried about my safety, maybe you can go on a tour or two with us."

Jared cocked an eyebrow. "I'm sure I can be convinced to do that ... given the right sort of persuasion, of course."

"What did you have in mind?"

"He's being perverted, Harp," Zander offered, sitting in the middle of the mess and opening a bag. "He wants you to do something dirty to convince him."

Jared bit back a sigh, his agitation growing with every word. "You make me tired."

"Right back at you." Zander was unruffled. "We're ordering pizza, right?"

"And wings," Harper said. "Oh, and cheesy bread. How about some of those brownies they make, too?"

Jared chuckled. "Are you hungry? Didn't you eat lunch?"

"We did, but we ran into Marley Winstead while we were there and the entire thing gave me indigestion."

"Marley Winstead?" Jared racked his brain. "Henry Spencer's granddaughter? I think Carol mentioned her daughter's name was Marley."

"Yeah, they were at the diner when we went for chili," Zander said. "That little monster knew about her grandfather's death and almost sounded happy about it."

"Happy?"

"She said that he was mean and we should know that because he always talked about us," Harper explained. "Apparently he was convinced that Zander was faking being gay and we were living in a *Three's Company* sort of situation."

Jared barked out a laugh, genuinely amused. "That's kind of funny."

"It was funny," Harper agreed, bobbing her head. "What wasn't funny was listening to Marley talk about her grandfather. She said he was mean to her, she wasn't sorry he was dead, and she was having a good day because she thought he was going to leave something good to her in his will."

Jared's smile slipped. "That doesn't sound very nice."

"She was definitely a pill," Zander agreed. "I had to drag Harper out of there before she smacked that kid around."

"Is that why you went shopping?" Shawn asked.

"No. We were always going to shop."

"Well, it looks as if you did a good job at it." Shawn turned his attention back to the menu. "So we need pizza, wings, cheesy bread, and brownies, right?"

"And a salad," Zander added. "I'm watching my figure for my costume this year." His eyes gleamed as he focused on Jared. "You might want to do the same."

Jared heaved out a sigh. "I just knew it."

JARED AND HARPER FELL INTO SOMETHING AKIN TO A food coma after eating dinner and drinking Zander's promised chocolate martinis. Despite the way the day started, it ended with a lot of laughter and flirty smiles between both couples.

Given how weary she felt when climbing into bed, Harper couldn't help being surprised when she woke for no apparent reason in the middle of the night. She spared a glance for Jared, who lightly snored as he happily slumbered away in the spot next to her.

Harper rubbed her cheek as she sat up, rolling her neck as she glanced around the room. She had no idea why she was awake given the fact that she was exhausted and yet she couldn't shake the feeling that she was missing something.

"Good evening," Jack announced, materializing at the end of the bed.

Harper nearly jumped out of her skin when she saw him. "What are you doing here?" she hissed, furious. "We're asleep. I've told you about just popping into my bedroom. We've had this talk before."

"We have," Jack agreed. "Don't worry. I made sure you weren't naked before visiting. I checked very thoroughly."

"That doesn't make things better."

"Who are you talking to?" Jared murmured, shifting. "If Zander is in here, I'm going to beat the snot out of him."

"It's not Zander."

"Okay."

"It's Jack."

Jared didn't open his eyes. "Jack the ghost?"

"Yes."

"Tell him to shut up and get out."

"I'm working on it."

"Okay." Jared absently patted Harper's arm. "I'm going back to sleep."

Harper tamped down her limited patience and fixed Jack with a hard look. "What are you doing here? It's the middle of the night."

"Yes, but I found a friend wandering outside and figured you would want to talk to him," Jack said. "He's the man you were looking for earlier."

Harper racked her brain. "Henry? You found Henry's ghost."

Jack nodded, solemn. "He seems a bit bamboozled."

"I think you're using that word wrong," Harper groused. "Can't you bring him back tomorrow? I'll have plenty of time for him during daylight hours. Then you and I can go over the rules about popping into my bedroom again."

"I think you should talk to him now," Jack said, refusing to back down. "He has something important to say."

"Fine." Harper blew out a sigh, resigned. "Where is he?"

"Right here." Jack motioned with his hand and Henry stepped forward, materializing out of the murk.

Harper pressed her lips together as she regarded him. "Mr. Spencer, I'm so sorry about your death. How are you feeling?"

For his part, Henry was positively flummoxed. "Why are you in bed with that one? I thought you were with the other one."

"Zander and I are just friends."

"Oh, please." Henry rolled his eyes. "I know he was faking that ... ailment. He didn't want anyone to know what he was really doing."

"It's not an ailment and I'm not in the mood to put up with your attitude if you're going to be difficult," Harper warned. "Zander is perfect the way he is and we've always been friends. The sooner you accept that, the better."

Henry opened his mouth to argue, but Jack shook his head to cut him off.

"Now, I believe you have something you want to talk about." Harper smoothed the front of her T-shirt, frowning when she caught sight of a spot of dried pizza sauce. "Did you have a message you want me to send to your daughter? Is that why you remained behind?"

"I remained behind because I was murdered and I want justice!" Henry barked out.

Harper's heart stuttered. "You were murdered, huh? Do you know who did it?" She wanted to crow about being right, but she wisely kept her euphoria to herself.

"I do know." Henry nodded sagely. "I know the who, where, and why. Why else do you think I'm here?"

"I think we both know the where," Harper replied dryly. "Let's go with the who. Who killed you?"

"It was assassins ... and they're not done. They're going to wipe out everybody. It's the end of the world as we know it."

"Oh, well, of course." Harper blew out a sigh. "He's crazy. That should make things easier."

SEVEN

"I'm sorry but ... assassins?"

Jared sipped his coffee the next morning, sparing a glance for Zander as Harper's roommate cooked a huge breakfast.

"Oh, don't do that." Harper wrinkled her forehead. "I already know it sounds ridiculous. You don't have to look to Zander for support."

"I wasn't looking to Zander for support. I was merely wondering when breakfast would be finished."

"Yeah, nobody believes that," Zander said. "You ate enough for two people last night. You're clearly not in danger of starving."

Jared scowled. "You make me want to smack you around at times. You know that, right?"

Zander grinned. "It's what I live for."

"Go back to the assassins," Shawn instructed. "I'm curious what that means."

Harper shrugged, helpless. "I don't know what it means. I tried to get more details, but he was all over the place. He said that masked assassins snuck into his house and killed him while he was watching reruns of *Alias* on Netflix."

Jared licked his lips, unsure how to proceed. "Have you considered that he believes assassins were in the house simply because he was watching *Alias*?"

"No, it never entered my ditzy brain," Harper deadpanned. "Of course I thought that. I even mentioned it to him, which you would know if you'd stayed awake to listen."

Jared refused to go down that route. "I can't hear what ghosts say to you. Whenever I try to be active in a conversation like that, you spend half your time repeating things for me and it slows things down. I thought it would be better to let you talk by yourself and then share information with me after the fact."

"And that had nothing to do with the fact that you ate your weight in pizza and wings last night, right?"

"Of course not."

"Or the fact that you don't believe Henry died from anything other than natural causes, right?" Harper pressed.

Jared ran his tongue over his teeth as he debated how to answer. "What do you want me to say here?" he challenged finally. "No matter what I say, it's not going to make you happy. If I tell the truth, then it's going to turn into a thing. If I lie, you'll know it's a lie and it's going to turn into a different thing. There's really no way for me to win here."

Harper took pity on him. "I'm sorry." She briefly leaned her forehead against his shoulder. "They kept me up for hours. I'm tired and taking it out on you. That's not fair."

Jared pressed a kiss to her forehead. "It's okay. I'm sorry I didn't realize you were up all night. You should've pinched me until I paid attention."

"No, I didn't want to bother you. I took them out into the living room so you wouldn't be disturbed. It's on me."

Jared shifted in his seat. "You left the bed?" He didn't like that he wasn't aware that happened. "I'm sorry. I should've been more alert."

Zander rolled his eyes. "She clearly wasn't in any danger. There's no reason to turn into Morose Man."

"Morose Man?"

"Yes, you're able to leap tall buildings with a single pout," Zander replied. "That's your superpower when you turn into Morose Man, by the way. That's why he's one of the lesser known superheroes."

"Good to know."

"Yes, I'm full of fascinating trivia." Zander placed several sausage links in a frying pan. "Did Henry say anything else about the assassins?"

Harper shook her head. "He just kept telling the story over and over again. It didn't change. He was watching *Alias*, became aware people were in the house, and by the time he tried to fight he was already incapacitated."

Jared decided to approach it how he would any case. "Incapacitated how?"

Harper shrugged. "He said he felt as if his muscles were full of fire and he couldn't move his body even though he tried to make it to the phone to call for help."

"Okay, and what did the assassins do after that? Did they ransack the house? Why would assassins be after him in the first place?"

"I honestly don't know," Harper replied. "He said he knew things that other people would want to know – and then he said he couldn't tell me what those things were because I didn't have security clearance – and it was obvious some foreign government sent assassins out to keep him quiet."

"I see." Jared didn't remotely see but he was keen to avoid a fight. "Did he mention which foreign government would want him dead?"

"He said it was probably the Russians, but he wouldn't rule out North Korea."

"Well, great." Jared scratched at the back of his neck. "Heart, I know you don't want to consider this, but is there a chance Henry was suffering from dementia before he died?"

Harper wrapped her hands around her coffee mug and shrugged. "I don't know. I guess there's always a possibility for anything."

"Except the Loch Ness Monster," Zander offered helpfully. "That one has been officially ruled out. I saw it on television."

Jared scowled. "Thank you so much for your contribution to this conversation."

"You're welcome."

Jared shifted his hand to Harper's back and absently rubbed it. She seemed tense and he wasn't sure how to make her feel better. "Do you believe that assassins killed your neighbor, sweetheart?"

Harper made a face only a mother could love. Not her mother, of course. Her mother would lecture her about frown lines and perhaps point out there was a possibility her face could freeze like that. Other mothers would find it adorable, though. "Do you think I believe assassins are to blame?"

"I don't know how to answer that," Jared replied after a beat. "I want to be the sort of boyfriend who always backs you up. If you believe assassins killed your neighbor, though, I'm going to have to adjust my brain to a new way of thinking."

Harper wanted to admonish him – or at least say something snarky – but all she could muster was a smile. "You're a wonderful boyfriend. Don't think otherwise."

"Thank you."

"And, no, I don't think assassins killed Henry," she continued. "I don't know what happened, but I'm trying to think like a rational person. I know you don't always believe I'm capable of that, but I'm doing my best."

"I think you're dropping a few of your doubts on me and that's not fair," Jared countered. "I don't for a second think you're ever irrational – well, except for when you and Zander decide you're making blueberry margaritas in the blender and get completely soused, but that happened once – and I know you have a solid mind. I always believe what you tell me. I need you to know that."

Harper's heart warmed at his earnest expression. "Thank you."

"You're welcome. That being said, it wasn't assassins."

Harper's mouth tipped down into a frown. "I know that."

"I think Henry probably had dementia, or at least the beginnings of it, and perhaps he had a stroke or heart attack and couldn't move. While on the floor, his mind played tricks on him, and he turned what was happening on the television into something he thought was happening in real life."

"Do you think that's really true?" Harper looked hopeful. "Do you think it's all in his head?"

"Can you think of another explanation?"

Harper honestly couldn't. "No. I feel bad for him, though. He seems almost rabid in his belief that it was assassins."

"I know you feel bad for him." Jared kneaded his fingers into Harper's tense neck. "You have the biggest heart of anyone I know. That doesn't mean he's telling the truth. Heck, he's probably not purposely lying. I'm going to guess he doesn't know that's not the truth."

"So what am I supposed to do?"

Jared shrugged. "I don't know, Heart. You're the ghost expert. Haven't you dealt with something like this before?"

"Usually ghosts don't turn crazy until they've been left to their own devices for decades," Harper explained. "When that happens I have no choice but to trap them in a dreamcatcher and send them on their way."

"Well, maybe that's what you should do with Henry."

"But ... he's new."

"Yes, but he also sounds as if he's suffering," Jared pointed out. "Do you want him to suffer?"

"No," Harper conceded. "I don't want to send him on his way before it's time, though, either."

"Harper, he was found dead in his living room with the television on. Nothing was taken. The house wasn't torn apart. There was no blood or wounds. He died of natural causes."

Harper wasn't ready to let it go. "Then why is he a ghost?"

"Because he's confused. I think the easiest answer is most often the correct answer."

Harper scratched the side of her nose. "I know in my head you're right, but he seemed so sincere. I don't want to discard everything he has to say because you think he's crazy."

Jared was about to argue when he thought better of it. If Harper wanted to hunt down invisible assassins that was better than having her chase real world murderers. "I think you should do what feels right. If you think that means letting Henry hang around a bit longer so you can talk to him, that's completely up to you."

Harper rolled her eyes. "Now you're just trying to placate me."

"I'm not. This is your gig and I don't want you doing anything that doesn't sit well with you. Once you send him over, you can't bring him back, right?"

"Right."

"So ... talk to him." Jared warmed to the idea. If Harper focused all her energy on something that couldn't possibly hurt her, that would give him time to figure out a solution to their living situation. It was the best of both worlds. "If he was suffering from dementia in life but still managed to live on his own without anyone noticing, that means he was probably coherent most of the time. You might get lucky and find him mentally fit the next time you guys get a chance to chat."

"Do you really think so?" Harper was hopeful.

"I definitely think it's worth a shot."

"I guess we have a plan then," Zander said. "Maybe Henry's ghost will see us decorating this afternoon and come for a visit. Then we'll be able to do two things at once."

"See." Jared beamed. "Zander has the right idea. Just ... see what happens."

"Fine. I will."

Great."

"DO YOU THINK Jared was shining me on?"

Two hours later, Harper and Zander were knee-deep in their new cemetery, but Harper couldn't completely push their breakfast conversation out of her mind.

"Oh, you're such a whiner this week." Zander planted his hands on his hips. "How long is this going to last?"

Harper had to bite her tongue to refrain from pointing out that Zander was a whiner twice as often as she was. "I'm not being a whiner. It was a legitimate question."

"It might be a legitimate question, but you're still being a whiner," Zander shot back. "If I knew you were going to be this much of a whiner when we hooked up in kindergarten, I might have showered Misty Dennis with my affection rather than you."

Harper snorted. "Please. Misty Dennis wears socks with sandals. You could never put up with that."

"I would've trained her to avoid doing that."

"Trained her?"

"I trained you, didn't I?"

Harper wanted to argue with the sentiment, but she was legitimately worried Zander did train her and it was too horrible to spend too much time considering. "Whatever. I'm not whining. I'm just ... unsure what to do. I've never been in a situation like this before."

Zander's expression softened. "Jared is right about you having a big heart. I've tried to drum that out of you, but you never listen. You're such a pain."

"Yes, and you're the easiest person in the world to get along with," Harper drawled. "I'm being serious here. What should I do about Henry?"

"I know you don't want to hear it, but I happen to agree with Jared on this one. There's no way assassins came to Whisper Cove and killed Henry Spencer. I mean ... what did he even do for a living? I've been trying to remember, but all I come up with is images of him during his retirement."

"He worked for the city."

"How do you remember that?"

"He stopped by the house for some reason – I can't remember exactly why – when I was in high school and my parents fought about it for weeks. Something about something they had to do for the house. I should've realized then they were going to get divorced."

"You did realize then," Zander pointed out. "You thought they were merely holding on until college. Then you thought they were only waiting until you graduated from college. After that you thought they would stay together because that's what they kept doing and they were too lazy to do anything else. They waited for you to give up the idea and then they smacked you over the head with it."

"You're not wrong," Harper acknowledged. "Still, I know you're probably also right about Henry. I think he's definitely confused, but that doesn't mean he died of natural causes. It's possible something else happened and he's confused about that."

"Okay, let's play the 'we're rational people' game," Zander

suggested. "What could have happened to him that explains everything you saw at that house?"

"I'm dying to hear the answer to that question, too," Henry announced, popping into existence at Harper's elbow and causing her to tilt to the side in surprise. "I want to know how I died."

Harper landed on the ground between fake tombstones with a thud, her eyes narrow slits as she glared at Henry. "You have got to learn to knock ... or at least make a noise before you scare the wits out of someone." She ruefully rubbed her rear end as she glanced to Zander. "Henry is here."

"I figured." Zander wasn't bothered by news that a ghost was visiting. "Tell him to stay out of your bedroom."

"I know. Jared doesn't like it."

"I don't care about Jared. If I can't be in there, though, he definitely can't be in there. It's simply unfair."

"I'll keep that I mind." Harper rolled her eyes until they landed on Henry. "Have you come to give me more information about how you died?"

Henry shook his head. "It was assassins. I told you that last night. Are you so slow you need me to keep repeating it to you?"

Harper puckered her mouth. "If you want me to help, you're going to have to be nicer to me. I don't need to be insulted."

"Yeah." Zander bobbed his head like a chicken as he stared into thin air. "We don't need your insults."

Henry rolled his eyes. "I can see why you don't want to be with this one. He's a dandy if I ever saw one."

Harper folded her arms over her chest. "I'm not kidding. You have to be nice if you want me to help."

"Fine." Henry's eyes fired as he held up his hands in mock surrender. "I promise to be nice."

"Good. Now, tell me about what you saw the night you died." Most ghosts were traumatized by death for days – sometimes even weeks – after their passing. Henry seemed invigorated by his death and only traumatized by real-life issues he couldn't quite relinquish. "We need to know where to look if we're going to find answers for you."

"It was assassins," Henry said succinctly.

Harper bit back a curse. "It wasn't assassins. Something else happened."

"No, it was assassins. I was there. Are you calling me a liar?"

"What is he saying?" Zander asked, only half listening to the conversation as he organized tombstones.

"He's back to the assassin thing."

"Tell him we're not helping unless he changes his story. People will think we're crazy if we start asking questions about assassins."

"I'm pretty sure half the town already believes we're crazy," Harper pointed out. "Is seeing ghosts much different than believing assassins killed someone?"

"That's a very good point." Henry beamed. "You're smarter than you look. That's a complete and total relief."

Harper scorched him with a dark look. "I'm at my limit with you. I'm not joking."

"Well, something tells me you'll survive." Henry was matter-of-fact. "I'm the dead one. That means my needs are more important than your needs."

Harper balked. "Says who?"

"Me."

"I didn't agree to those terms."

"Well, you have to. I need help and it appears you're my only chance of getting it. If you don't willingly do it, I'll have to think of other means to get my way."

Harper wasn't about to be bullied. "Like what?"

"Did I mention I sing? I'm a big fan of musicals."

That was too much for anyone to bear. "Fine. We'll help. Where should we start?"

"How should I know? You're the experts."

And just like that, Ghost Hunters, Inc. was on the case ... and they had no idea where to look first.

8

EIGHT

With no idea where to point herself, Harper left Zander to fuss over the Halloween decorations and opted for a visit with Carol. Zander wasn't happy about being abandoned, but he agreed to do the heavy lifting if Harper brought back lunch so it was a compromise of sorts.

Carol answered the door with a harried look on her face, pulling up short when she saw Harper on the other side of the threshold. Harper thought ahead and stopped at the local market for a comfort dish – opting for a shepherd's pie that Carol could stick in the oven and serve for dinner – and she adopted a sympathetic smile.

"I ... what are you doing here?" Carol asked, confused.

"I thought I would stop by and offer my condolences. I brought something easy for you to make for dinner."

"Oh, well, thank you." Carol's expression softened as she took the dish and ushered Harper inside. "I didn't mean to be so rude. It's just ... I never knew how much work went along with a death. I guess I should have – I remember my father complaining about it when my mother died – but it's a lot."

Harper decided the easiest way to get Carol talking was by offering her services. "What can I do to help?"

"Oh, you're so sweet. You don't need to help, though. It's not your responsibility."

"I want to help. If I go home, I have to help Zander with the Halloween decorations. Give me a job."

"Are you sure?" Carol remained unconvinced.

"Absolutely. I feel as if I knew your father relatively well because we lived next door to him for so long."

Instead of falling for Harper's line of bull, Carol merely snorted. "Honey, I know my father was terrible to you. He did nothing but complain about you and Zander whenever I visited. He even had binoculars to watch you because he was convinced that you were doing something illegal and he was going to catch you."

Harper was both mortified and amused. "Did he ever see us doing anything illegal?"

"He swears you were having orgies."

Harper's eyebrows flew up her forehead. "Orgies?"

"He didn't understand about Zander being gay. He thought you were dating three men, even though I tried explaining that new one – the one from the gym – was there for Zander. Everyone knew you and Jared were together, but he was convinced you were dating all three of them."

"That's either extremely flattering or really insulting."

"I would be flattered. He said I was too fat to attract a husband after David and I divorced."

Now Harper was offended on Carol's behalf. "He said that to you?"

"He didn't mean anything by it. He was blunt. He said the worst thing I ever did was divorce David even though he was cheating on me."

Harper tilted her head to the side, searching her memory. "I guess I forgot about that part. David moved to Sterling Heights, didn't he? I never see him around here any longer."

"Yes, he has a new wife and a son. He barely calls Marley on her birthday."

Even though her parents were genuine pains – and currently embroiled in the world's longest divorce – Harper couldn't imagine either of them abandoning her without contact. There were times she wished her mother would consider it, but it was one of those frustrated inner pleas that she didn't really mean.

"That must be hard for Marley." Harper sat on the couch and accepted the soda Carol handed her. It seemed their work afternoon was turning into a gossip session, which was exactly what Harper wanted. "Does she talk about her father?"

"She did at first. We've been divorced for three years. Now she goes out of her way not to talk about him. I think that's almost more painful."

"I bet." Harper popped the top on the Diet Coke. "I saw Marley yesterday. She was in the diner when Zander and I were finishing up lunch."

"Oh, really?" Carol seemed surprised. "What was she doing there? I told her to come straight home after school because of her grandfather. I thought we should talk in case she had any questions ... or wanted to have a good cry."

"She was with a boy. Zander said his name is Mike Dunlap."

"Oh, right." Carol made a face. "He's the quarterback of the football team. He's all Marley talks about. I never thought I would raise a boy-crazy daughter – in fact, that's the exact opposite of what I wanted to do – but it turns out that I did.

"My father gave me grief about that, too," she continued. "I tried telling him that teenagers – especially girls – can't seem to help themselves, but he didn't listen. I wasn't as boy crazy as Marley, but I learned to hide it well when I was a teenager because I knew he would melt down over it."

"My mother didn't think I was boy crazy enough," Harper supplied. "She thought my friendship with Zander was a detriment to me ever finding a boyfriend. Before Jared, I think she believed I was hopeless."

"Oh, see, I always knew you would find someone eventually. I thought that might cause a rift with Zander because he's so picky – I mean the stories about him ditching dates in the middle of restaurants are legendary – but he seems to have found someone, too."

"Shawn. He's great. He's extremely calm and doesn't fly off the handle about anything. That is exactly the sort of boyfriend Zander needs."

"According to my father, you all slept in the same bed. Is that true?"

Harper widened her eyes. "Not last time I checked. It's usually Jared and me in one bed and Zander and Shawn in another."

"I told him he was seeing things. He kept pointing his binoculars at your bedroom and swore up and down that you, Jared and Zander were in there together every morning."

Harper shifted on her seat, uncomfortable. "Well ... technically Zander comes for the occasional visit, but it's only in the mornings when he wants to gossip and nobody is doing anything funny."

Instead of being offended, Carol barked out a laugh that caught Harper off guard. "Oh, he was right. I thought for sure he was full of it. It kind of makes me sad that he was right because I can't apologize."

"I'm sure he feels he was right so it doesn't matter regardless," Harper said, lifting a catalog from the coffee table. "What's this?"

"Coffin stuff. My father left specific instructions for his burial needs, and they included a coffin pillow. I'm trying to pick one out."

"That's not morbid or anything," Harper complained, opening the catalog. "Do you have a preference on color?"

"Red. His coffin lining is red, also specific to his instructions. He said white, gray, and cream stained too easily. I tried explaining that he would be dead so it didn't matter, but he refused to listen. He was always a pain that way."

"My parents are pains, too," Harper said. "When they die, I'm sure there will be all sorts of kooky things going on. Your father sounds a lot like my mother."

"He was just ... set in his ways," Carol explained.

"You don't have to defend him to me. I didn't talk to him a lot, but he was never overtly mean or anything."

"That's only because you couldn't hear the things he was saying behind your back. Trust me. He was really mean and he said some awful things about you and Zander. In fact, I feel guilty for you even caring enough to stop by. He wouldn't have done the same for you."

Harper didn't doubt that for a second. "That doesn't matter to me. I can't control the actions of others. You're not mean. I'll simply think of it as helping you."

"That's a nice thought." Carol smiled. "He really wasn't a bad guy.

He just believed life should be lived a certain way. I often think he was obsessive-compulsive, although they didn't really diagnose that for people back in his day. That's always what I thought, though."

Harper searched her memory for incidents with Henry that would prove Carol's theory, smiling when one popped into her mind. "Once he called Mel because the bushes in front of our house weren't even. The middle one was taller than the others. That was on purpose because Zander decided to make our yard something everyone would talk about. It turned out only your father noticed ... and he wasn't happy."

"That came from his days as a code enforcement officer," Carol supplied. "He thought that all bushes should be the exact same height and melted down whenever he saw something uneven. I think that's where code enforcement and obsessive-compulsive disorder collided."

"Huh." The theory made sense to Harper. "You know, I have a memory of him stopping by my parents' house when I was in high school. They fought long and hard after – it was something about the garage – and I never understood why your father's visit coincided with a fight. I guess I do now."

"Do you want to know what's really sad?" Carol's smile was rueful. "I know what he cited your parents for because he told me. He used to tell me about all of them."

"What was it?"

"The trim on the garage didn't match the trim on the house. It was one color off – ecru instead of eggshell – and he was massively upset about it."

Harper snorted, genuinely amused. "Oh, that sounds right. My father painted the trim not long after."

"Most people in code enforcement spend their time looking at overgrown yards, cars parked on bricks in the front yard, things that could draw rats, and other stuff like that," Carol volunteered. "My father cited all those things, but he went after the little things, too. That's why the bulk of people in town hated him."

"Oh, I don't think that's true."

"No, it's true." Carol was adamant. "Do you know how many citations he gave out during his years with the town?"

"Um ... I'm not sure anyone could possibly know that."

"He did. He kept track. He gave out one hundred thousand and one citations. He told anyone who would listen about that and he was annoyed because he purposely stayed on the job until he could hit the big round number of one hundred thousand. Once he did it he was on his way back to the office to hang up his ticket pad and then he saw a woman with mismatched garbage containers and added another citation to his last day. That extra citation drove him crazy and yet he couldn't stop himself from writing it."

Harper was flabbergasted. "Oh, wow."

"Yeah, he had a few issues." Carol let loose with a sigh and pinched the bridge of her nose. "He was a pain in the butt and yet I loved him. I have no idea why I'm telling you this but ... you're the only one who seems to care."

Harper's heart went out to the woman. "Parents are often difficult without realizing they're being that way. My parents drive me crazy, but I love them. I can't imagine losing both of them."

"There's nothing I can change about that, though. I simply have to move forward."

"Then I'll help you move forward." Harper forced a smile. "So, we need to start with a pillow, right? I like this one." Harper pointed to an image in the catalog. "It's got pizzazz."

"Funnily enough, that's the one I liked, too. I think we have a winner."

"WHAT ARE YOU DOING?"

Mel flicked an annoyed look in Jared's direction as they drove past Harper's house. His partner's eyes were glued outside the passenger window and Mel couldn't stop the frustration from bubbling up. Jared had been distracted all day.

"Zander is in the yard by himself and Harper's car is gone."

Mel failed to see the issue. "So?"

"So she's not there."

"I figured that out myself and I didn't even need to dust off my trusty detective's badge. Why is that an issue?"

Jared rolled his neck as he focused on his partner. "Because she's acting weird."

"I'm going to need more information than that. Harper often acts weird."

"She does not. She's a unique soul and she's perfect all around."

Mel heaved out a sigh. "You can't have it both ways, son. You can't complain about her in one breath and stand up for her with the next. You need to pick an emotion so I can follow the conversation."

"I'm not complaining. It's just ... I know you don't want to hear this stuff, but I need to talk about it. I'm going to ignore your rules and go for it. If you don't like it ... well ... suck it up. I have no choice."

"Oh, well, you've got me intrigued now." Mel cracked a smile. "What do I have to suck up?"

"Okay, so, we were in bed last night ... ."

"Hold the phone." Mel held up his hand to still Jared. "I am not listening to crazy sex talk. I was very clear about that."

Jared scowled. "Do you really think I want to talk to you about that?"

"That's what it sounds like."

"Well, you're wrong." Jared sucked in a breath. "We were in bed and two ghosts came to visit."

"Oh, geez." Mel made a face as he turned toward the police station. "Why do you have to share this information with me? You know I don't like talking about the ghosts."

"I do know that," Jared confirmed. "I don't care, though. It's bugging me and now you're going to have to deal with it. One of the ghosts was Henry Spencer."

Mel cocked an eyebrow, intrigued despite himself. "I see. And what did Henry Spencer have to say from the great beyond? Wait, let me guess, he was murdered and he knows who did it."

"He does claim he was murdered. He doesn't know exactly who did it, but he's convinced it was assassins."

Mel snorted so hard he coughed up a ball of phlegm and made Jared cringe. "I'm sorry but ... what?"

"Oh, don't take that tone." Jared realized he sounded exactly like Harper when she said the same words to him over breakfast. "Harper doesn't believe it was assassins, but she's convinced Henry is hanging around for a reason."

"And what do you think?"

"I think there's a very good chance Henry was suffering from some form of dementia and his ghost is as confused as the flesh-and-blood man was on occasion. I mean ... it couldn't be anything else."

"Huh. That's a good theory." Mel stroked his chin. "What did Harper say to that explanation?"

"It's not what she said that bothers me. It's what she didn't say."

"And what didn't she say?"

"She said all the right things," Jared replied. "She doesn't believe it's assassins."

"But?"

"But she's still convinced Henry was killed and even though she won't admit it, I can't quite shake the belief out of her. I don't know what to do."

"Well, we should be getting the ruling from the medical examiner any minute. In fact, he said he would text before noon and that's only twenty minutes away. Once we have science to back us up, she's going to be hard pressed to argue with the findings."

"I want to believe that, but she's convinced she needs to help Henry."

"Well, I don't know what to tell you," Mel said. "The good news is, I doubt very much assassins are running around so she's going to be safe for a change. That's good news, right?"

"Sadly, that was the first thing that jumped into my head. I can't help feeling guilty about it."

Mel's expression was rueful as he parked behind the station. "I forgot how dramatic young love can be. My wife and I have been married so long the only source of drama in our house is who gets up to get the popcorn on movie nights."

Jared rolled his eyes. "She's not being dramatic just to be dramatic."

"I didn't say she was." Mel looked down when his phone dinged with an incoming message. "I bet that's the medical examiner. In thirty seconds you'll have proof Henry wasn't murdered and hopefully enough gumption to talk Harper down from a ledge."

"You seem pretty sure of yourself."

"I am." Mel focused on his phone, furrowing his brow when he finished reading the message. "Huh."

"What?" Jared was instantly alert.

"I so don't want to tell you this, but I don't see where I have a choice."

"I'm waiting."

"It seems Henry Spencer didn't die from natural causes. He was poisoned."

All the oxygen whooshed out of Jared's lungs. "Hah! She was right! You owe her a huge apology."

"Oh, geez," Mel complained, rubbing his forehead. "I'm never going to live this down, am I?"

"Nope. Not even a little."

"That's what I thought."

Jared was triumphant for a full thirty seconds and then he sobered. "What do we do now?"

9

NINE

Harper returned home with lunch, related her morning to Zander, and then convinced him to head to the senior center with her. Carol didn't have a lot of tidbits, but one of the more interesting ones involved her father's "friends" at the senior center.

"So, wait," Zander said, holding up a hand to still Harper in the center's parking lot. He was still trying to wrap his head around a few things. "Henry had no friends and ticked off everyone he knew but still hung with the old folks here?"

Harper glanced around to make sure no one overheard the statement. "I don't think you're supposed to call them 'old folks.' Some of them might find it rude."

Zander rolled his eyes. "They're folks and they're old. What do you want from me?"

Harper made an exasperated sound in the back of her throat. "Just ... don't be a pain when we're in there. We can't get information from people if they think we're rude."

"Um ... I'll have you know that people happen to think I'm a delight," Zander argued. "Old people especially love me. They find me whimsical."

Harper furrowed her brow. "Since when?"

"Since forever."

"That's not exactly how I remember it."

"Oh, really? How do you remember it?" Zander adopted a challenging stance, folding his arms over his chest as he regarded his best friend with a dubious look.

"Well, for example, we donated our time at the retirement home that one Christmas before college because we needed to add stuff to our transcripts for admissions and we were barred from ever returning because you dyed Madge Harrington's hair blue and her daughter was not impressed."

"Oh, that was a mistake," Zander argued, his irritation coming out to play. "She said she wanted beautiful hair and I assumed she meant that I could decide what was beautiful – mostly because she was too blind to do it herself. It's not my fault that she had no vision."

"You also tried to get her to wear satin leggings and a push-up bra."

"And those were fine choices."

"Whatever." Harper shook her head. "I need you to be on your best behavior. I wouldn't have brought you if I thought you were going to serve as a distraction."

Zander didn't believe that for a second. "You like it when I'm a distraction."

Harper wanted to argue, but all she could do was smile. "Sometimes," she conceded after a beat. "Today, though, we're undercover and trying to find out information on Henry. We need a direction to look and he was a loner other than the time he spent with these people. That means we have to ingratiate ourselves with them."

Zander flicked her ear. "I guess it's good for you that I'm a professional ingratiator, huh?"

Harper wrinkled her nose. "I don't think that's a real word."

"It is."

"I'm going to look it up when we get home."

"I'm looking forward to it."

"I DON'T UNDERSTAND."

Carol barely had a chance to return to her work after Harper's departure before there was another knock at the door. This time Harper's boyfriend was on the other side and Carol's confusion was complete.

"I know this is hard to grasp," Mel said, gently putting his hand to Carol's elbow and prodding her to sit. "The medical examiner is certain, though. Your father didn't die from natural causes."

"And someone poisoned him?" Carol struggled to wrap her head around the statement. "But ... how?"

"We're not sure yet," Mel replied. "We're going to head over to his house again this afternoon and take a look around."

"I thought you already did that?"

"We did, but the search was cursory because we assumed Henry died of a heart attack or stroke," Mel replied, choosing his words carefully. "This search will be more in depth."

"Because he was poisoned."

"Exactly."

"But ... how?"

Jared took pity on the woman as he sat in the chair across from her and rubbed his hands against his knees. He felt bad for her – her confusion and disbelief were understandable, after all – but they needed to get her to a point of understanding before leaving.

"We're still not sure how it was done," Jared replied. "We know that he was poisoned by arsenic. We're going to search the house for sources when we get there."

"But ... arsenic?" Carol furrowed her brow. "That's not just something you can accidentally stumble across, is it?"

"It's not common, but it does occasionally pop up organically in nature," Mel hedged. "It's in some algaecides and herbicides. It's also used in glass manufacturing. We're simply not sure how your father came into contact with it."

"You wouldn't be involved if you didn't think someone purposely poisoned him," Carol noted, her mind busy. "You think someone killed him and that's why you're here."

"The medical examiner said that the odds of your father accidentally ingesting enough arsenic to kill him are slim to none," Mel confirmed. "That means someone poisoned him. Do you have any idea who that would be?"

Carol balked. "Do you honestly think I would just sit back and do nothing if I thought someone was capable of poisoning my father?"

"Of course not," Mel said automatically. "We're looking for suspects, though. We have to start somewhere."

"Is this why Harper was here earlier?"

The question knocked Jared for a loop. "Excuse me?"

"Harper," Carol repeated. "She left about an hour ago. She said she stopped by to help – brought a shepherd's pie and everything – but she seemed more interested in asking questions about my father and his relationship with others than anything else."

Jared forced himself to remain calm. "Last time I checked, Harper didn't know that your father had been poisoned. We were still working under the 'natural causes' theory this morning and she said she was spending the day decorating with Zander."

"Oh." Carol scratched at her chin, unnerved. "Then why was she here?"

Jared had a sneaking suspicion he knew exactly why Harper visited Carol. He didn't give voice to that notion, though, instead holding his hands palms out. "I have no idea. I know she was upset thinking about your father dying alone. She probably just wanted to check on you because of that."

"But she asked a lot of questions."

Jared exchanged a quick look with Mel, something unsaid passing between them. "And what questions were those?"

"She wanted to know who my father hung out with, if he ever ticked off somebody so badly through work that he received threats, and whether my father had a secret girlfriend or watched too much television. Oh, she also wanted to know if he read a lot of books about assassins."

It took everything Jared had to remain calm. "I see." A muscle worked in his jaw as he tamped down his temper. "And what did you tell her?"

Carol shrugged, oblivious to Jared's fury as she worked through her own emotions. "I told her that my father ticked off everyone in town because he was with code enforcement and took his job very seriously."

"He definitely took his job seriously," Mel agreed. "He once ticketed me because the numbers on my mailbox weren't even. You know those stickers you buy? Yeah, one was slightly higher than the rest and it drove him batty."

Carol turned apologetic. "I think he had a touch of OCD."

Mel offered up a soothing pat on the shoulder. "I don't blame you. Even though I was angry at first, I had a good laugh about it after. Your father was a unique soul."

"He was," Carol agreed. "He wasn't easy to get along with, though."

"He definitely wasn't."

Carol's eyes widened as she realized something. "That's going to make your job harder, isn't it? You're going to have a lot of suspects. My father irritated so many people that I'm going to guess half the town wanted him dead at one time or another."

"I think that agitation over code violations turning to murder isn't normal for most people," Mel hedged. "I'm sure people were irritated, but most people wouldn't kill over it."

"Someone did."

"Someone killed your father for a very specific reason," Jared countered. "We don't yet know what that reason is. It might have something to do with his days on the code enforcement team or it might have to do with something else entirely."

"Do you really believe that?" Carol looked doubtful.

"We're not sure, but we need to go through some information with you," Mel answered. "We have some questions."

"Okay. What questions?"

"For starters, what exactly did you tell Harper?" Jared pressed. "What was she most interested in?"

If Carol found the question odd, she didn't mention it. "Well ... we spent a lot of time talking about old stories from when he was on the job and then it turned to stories about how he filled in occasionally after he retired. Oh, and then we talked about his friends at the senior center."

Jared's eyes lit with interest. "Yeah, tell me about the senior center."

HARPER AND ZANDER ZEROED IN ON A PARTICULAR table five minutes after strolling through the senior center's front door. They expected to be questioned about their presence, but no one so much as looked in their direction.

"Do you find it odd that no one has asked us if we're perverts?" Zander asked.

Harper shrugged. "I think it's weird when anyone doesn't ask if you're a pervert."

"Ha, ha." Zander elbowed her stomach. "You're so funny I forgot to laugh."

"Then why did you say 'ha, ha' like that?"

Zander frowned. "You're quick on the draw today. I don't like it."

"I don't like when anyone is quick on the draw," Harper teased, inclining her chin toward four visitors who seemed to be involved in a deep discussion. "I think we should hit that table first."

Zander followed her gaze. "You're just saying that because Annie Garrett is friends with my mother and you know she's a gossip."

"So?"

Zander shrugged. "I happen to love a gossip. I agree we should start there."

"Let's do it."

Annie Garrett, her bottle blond curls bright under the harsh senior center lights, did a double take when she found Harper and Zander standing at the edge of her table. "You're the Pritchett boy, right?"

Zander nodded and pasted a bright smile on his face. "I believe you're friendly with my mother."

"Yes, and you're the bane of her existence."

Zander's smile slipped. "My mother loves me more than anything. She tells me whenever we talk on the phone."

"Then she's lying to you." Annie flicked her eyes to Harper. "And you're the Harlow girl, right?"

Harper swallowed hard. "I am." She had a feeling Annie was about to say something mean and she braced herself for it.

"You're the one who can see ghosts, aren't you?"

Harper realized she should've expected that question. "I am. Do you have a problem with that?"

Annie shrugged, noncommittal. "I'm not sure I believe in ghosts."

"Well, I didn't say you had to believe in them."

"The older I get, though, the more I like the idea of sticking around so I can haunt people I don't like," Annie added. "I think you're probably interesting. Sit down."

Harper opened her mouth to argue with the invitation, but Annie's expression told her that was a bad idea. Instead of poking the woman, she sat between Glenn Lassiter and Carl Hill and flashed a pretty smile for both of them. "This seems like a fun group."

Glenn, who combed his hair over his bald spot and had spark plugs for eyebrows, merely smirked. "You're pretty."

"Thank you."

"How come you spend all of your time with a gay guy when you're so pretty?" Glenn challenged. "I thought gay guys were meant to hang out with ugly girls."

"Hey!" Zander was understandably offended. "I refuse to spend time with ugly people and I don't appreciate stereotypes."

Glenn chuckled. "You get worked up easy, don't you?"

"I happen to be even tempered," Zander shot back, opting to sit between Annie and Eve Nelson, scorching Glenn with a dark glare as he got comfortable. "I'm a complete joy to be around. Just ask my mother."

"Your mother says that you complain all the time and you're a tyrant when you don't get your way," Annie pointed out.

"You say that like it's a bad thing," Zander said dryly.

Annie snorted. "You may be high maintenance, but you're obviously funny. I like funny."

"Me, too." Glenn leered suggestively at Harper. "Are you funny?"

Harper fought the urge to smack him upside the head. "I'm a laugh riot." She knew she would have to focus the conversation if she wanted answers. "We're here about Henry Spencer."

Annie raised her eyebrows, surprised. "He's dead. News broke on that yesterday."

"Yes, but we're looking for information on him," Harper pressed. "We heard he hung here."

"Although I can't figure out why." Zander wrinkled his nose. "This place is depressing and the lighting is not flattering."

"Get used to being old," Carl suggested, a twinkle in his eye. "You don't care what you look like when you're old."

"Speak for yourself," Eve shot back. "I like feeling pretty."

Zander beamed at her. "A woman after my own heart."

Eve wrinkled her forehead. "I thought you were gay."

"Just ... forget it." Zander made a disgusted sound and focused on Harper. "Ask your questions. The faster we can get out of here, the better."

"You have questions?" Annie leaned forward, intrigued. "What kind of questions?"

"We're trying to find out more information on Henry," Harper replied. "I know that he was retired but still picked up a few shifts when workers were sick here and there. What else can you tell me about him?"

"There's not much else to tell," Carl answered. "He lived and breathed that job. Once his wife passed – and that was years ago, mind you – he never talked about anything but that job. It was all he cared about."

"What about Carol?" Harper asked. "She was his daughter. He must have talked about her."

"Oh, sure," Annie said. "He talked about how she couldn't hold on to her husband and what a disappointment she was."

Harper worked overtime to hide her annoyance. "Yeah. I was with Carol earlier. She mentioned something similar."

"He wasn't a good man," Annie said. "He wasn't evil by any stretch of the imagination, but he wasn't good either."

"You hung out with him here, though," Zander pointed out. "You must have liked him at least a little bit."

Glenn shrugged. "We like everybody." He waggled his eyebrows for Harper's benefit. "I especially like you, honey."

Harper extended a warning finger. "You may be old but that doesn't mean I won't start kicking if you decide to get handsy."

Glenn adopted an innocent expression. "Who says I'm going to get handsy?"

"He likes getting handsy," Annie said, shaking her head. "Watch him. He thinks he can get away with anything because he's old. We've told him otherwise, but he pretends he doesn't hear us."

"Yeah, he always says he left his hearing aid at home even though he doesn't need one," Eve added. "He's annoying."

Despite the situation, Harper couldn't stop herself from smiling. The four friends got along how she imagined she and Zander would sixty years in the future. It was somehow soothing to her, although she had no idea why.

"Go back to Henry," Zander prodded. "Do you know anyone who didn't like him?"

Carl let loose with a hearty laugh. "Nobody liked him."

"He must've had some friends," Harper pressed.

"He had acquaintances," Annie clarified. "We played cards with him occasionally, but only if we were forced because he liked to cheat when he thought no one was looking."

"He cheated at cards?" Zander was understandably offended. "I hate that."

"Join the club," Glenn said. "Although, if you want to cheat with me, honey, I would totally be open for it." He moved a lecherous hand in Harper's direction, but she smoothly grabbed him around the wrist and kept him from touching her.

"Don't make me hurt you," Harper warned. "I'll do it. I won't like it, but I'll do it."

"Leave the girl alone," Annie ordered, agitation evident. "She doesn't have to put up with your crap simply because she's young and you're her elder. Show her some respect."

The corners of Glenn's mouth tipped down. "You're absolutely no fun, Annie."

"I'm tons of fun," Annie shot back. "That doesn't mean I'm going to watch you molest that poor girl. She's done nothing to deserve it and you're a pig."

"Maybe you're a pig," Glenn muttered under his breath.

Annie ignored the pouting. "Listen, nobody liked Henry. Everyone hated him. We tolerated him because there was nothing more we could do. The organizers insist we be inclusive if we hang out."

"Did anyone especially hate him, though?" Harper asked.

Annie swished her lips back and forth. "I know you don't want to hear it, but everyone hated him. He was not a well-liked man."

"Can you give me some examples?"

"How much time do you have."

Harper spared a glance for Zander and found him staring back at her with mutinous eyes. Despite that, Harper heaved out a sigh. "Lay it on me."

Glenn's creepy grin was back. "I thought you'd never give me the go ahead, but I guess I was wrong."

Harper grabbed Glenn's thumb and gave it a good squeeze, causing him to make a face. "Don't push me too far."

Annie chuckled. "I'm starting to like you. Okay, we'll tell some stories. I'm not sure they're what you want to hear, though, but we'll give it a shot."

Harper smiled. "That's all I ask."

TEN

"What do you think?"

Harper and Zander took advantage of the pleasant afternoon and bought gourmet coffees from the downtown shop before sitting at one of the metal tables in town square. They spent two hours at the senior center, and the bevy of information they received was daunting to wade through.

"I think that Glenn was a complete and total jerk and I'm going to need to shower when we get home," Harper replied dryly.

"Not *that*. Although, yeah, he's disgusting. I wanted to break his hands. I mean about what they said."

"I'm not sure what to think," Harper said after a beat and a sip of pumpkin latte goodness. "It sounds as if Henry had zero friends and yet he insisted on visiting the senior center. I'm not sure what to make of that."

"I found the entire thing sad," Zander said. "I hope we don't end up like that."

"Really? I thought it was kind of fun. I can picture us sitting around messing with each other when we're that age."

"I could never hang out there." Zander was firm. "You know I prefer pink gels for my lighting."

"Not that part." Harper couldn't hold back a laugh. "I don't expect to hang out at the senior center. We'll hang out at our houses or other places. Still, I like the idea that we'll be just as close then as we are now."

Zander grinned. "I like that idea, too. Do you think it will really happen?"

"Why wouldn't it?"

"Because we won't always live together. What if we grow apart when we have separate houses?"

Harper found Zander's downtrodden expression amusing. "Do you think I'll lose interest in you if we don't share a roof?"

"I don't know. I think it's impossible for anyone to lose interest in me."

"I agree."

"Still, we spend a lot of time together," Zander hedged. "We're especially close because of it. What if the magic fades when we're in separate houses and instead of talking each day we only talk once a week ... and then once a month ... and then we'll become people who only talk around the holidays."

Harper stared at him blankly.

"It could happen," Zander pressed. "They make movies about it."

"We work together five days a week ... and sometimes on weekends. How is that going to happen?"

"I don't know. It could happen, though. I don't want to become the sort of people who only have one awkward conversation a year. In fact – yeah, we can't separate. I've given it some thought and we're simply going to have to get a house that's big enough for the four of us."

Harper couldn't stop herself from laughing. "You're so dramatic."

"That doesn't mean I'm wrong."

"You're totally wrong. That will never happen to us."

"How can you be sure?"

"Because I'm addicted to you ... and I love you ... and you're part of my very soul."

Zander pursed his lips, touched. "I love you, too. Still, all this upheaval makes me nervous. If I'm not careful, it's going to cause me to break out ... and no one wants that."

"We'll stop at the pharmacy for some tea tree oil on our way home," Harper said. "I promise your complexion will stay clear no matter what."

"I'm going to hold you to that." Zander shifted his neck before returning to the original point of conversation. "As for Henry, it sounds as if the guy was a real douche and almost everyone wanted him dead."

"Yeah, but idly thinking that your life would be better if someone died and actually killing him are two wildly different things."

"You sound like Jared."

"You say that like it's a bad thing."

Zander rolled his eyes. "It's sometimes a bad thing," he clarified. "Right now, though, we need to find a suspect who would have the inclination to kill Henry because he was a jerk. I mean ... what other motivation could there be?"

"I don't know." Harper opted for honesty. "Maybe we're missing something."

"Henry only had Carol left for family and you don't seem to think she's capable of killing her father."

"Definitely not."

"So ... who does that leave?"

Harper's eyes drifted to the park across the way, her gaze landing on Marley as the girl cavorted with her football player boyfriend. "There's one other family member."

Zander shifted so he could stare at the teenagers. "You can't be serious."

"I doubt it's her, but I wouldn't mind talking to her again. Maybe she was simply putting on a show yesterday."

"Okay, but I'm only agreeing because I enjoy standing next to teenage boys. It makes me realize how young I look ... and how glad I am that I'm mature enough to be out of high school."

Harper had doubts about the "maturity" claim but she kept them to herself. "Let's head over there. It might be nothing, but I want to be sure."

"Let's do it."

"WOW. OUTSIDE VISITORS TWICE IN ONE DAY." ANNIE looked Jared and Mel up and down with an unreadable expression. "How did we get so lucky?"

Jared kept his face placid as he glanced between faces. "I think it probably has something to do with your personality."

"Oh, you're so full of charm," Annie drawled. "I can see what that Harlow girl sees in you."

"I don't," Glenn said, folding his arms over his chest. "She clearly has terrible taste in men."

Jared was affronted. "Excuse me?"

Eve made a tsking sound with her tongue as she played a card. "Ignore him. He's upset because your girlfriend bent his finger back and made him cry like a schoolgirl. She left an hour ago and he's still pouting about it."

Jared had no idea what to do with the new information. "I see. Wait ... Harper bent your finger back?"

"My thumb." Glenn held up his hand for emphasis. "She's a mean little cuss."

Jared flicked his eyes to Annie for answers. "Do you want to explain?"

"Your girlfriend was here for two hours," Annie replied. "She had a bunch of questions."

"She also had that poof with her," Carl added.

Eve cuffed the back of the cranky man's head. "Don't use words like that. I happen to like Zander. He can't help the way he is. He was born that way."

"I don't believe that. I think that's a lie the media spreads to cover up for deviant behavior."

"You need to stop reading conspiracy blogs on the internet," Eve chided.

"Men in my day weren't like that," Carl argued.

"Yes, they were." Eve wasn't in the mood to listen to one of Carl's infamous diatribes. "They simply didn't tell anyone they were gay. They were – what do you call it? – closeted."

"Men in my time got married."

"That doesn't mean they weren't gay."

"It does so."

"It does not."

"It does so."

"It does not."

Mel cleared his throat to stop the argument. "Zander is a good boy and he didn't choose to be the way he is. Eve is right."

Eve's eyebrows flew up her forehead. "Ha!"

"He's just saying that to protect his family honor," Carl groused. "Gay people didn't become a thing until people forgot the old ways."

"You're such an idiot," Annie said, shaking her head. "Sit there and shut up until someone specifically addresses you. We'd all appreciate it."

"We would," Eve agreed.

Annie flicked her eyes to Mel. "Let me guess, you guys are here to ask questions about Henry Spencer, aren't you?"

"What makes you think that?" Jared asked, sitting between Carl and Glenn. The look he shot Glenn was straight out of a western movie, practically daring him to say something nasty about Harper.

"Because your girlfriend was asking about him and she seemed a bit intense," Annie replied.

"And mean." Glenn held up his thumb again. "She really hurt me."

"And why would she do that?" Jared asked.

"Because he groped her and wouldn't stop even though she warned him she wasn't above physical violence," Annie explained. "I wasn't sure about her when she first approached – you know, that ghost stuff is ridiculously weird and I thought she might be crazy – but I really like her now."

Jared licked his lips. "You groped my girlfriend?"

Glenn balked. "You didn't see the way she was dressed."

"She was wearing jeans, a T-shirt, and a coat," Eve said. "She wasn't dressed slutty or anything."

"Even if she was, that doesn't give you the right to touch her," Jared pointed out. "Harper has a right to make decisions for her own body."

"That's right," Carl teased. "No means no."

"That's not how it was in my day," Glenn groused.

"Yes, well that's how it is now," Jared said. "If you touch her again, I'm going to do more than bend your thumb back."

"I SEE WHERE SHE GETS HER AGGRESSION FROM," GLENN GRUMBLED.

"I'm far more aggressive than her," Jared warned. "That's not why we're here, though. We're here to talk about Henry."

"I don't see what we can tell you that we didn't already tell Harper," Annie said. "Henry was disliked by everyone and mean to anyone who would bother to spend time with him. He wasn't a pleasant guy and I know a lot of people who aren't crying any tears of sorrow over his death. Tears of joy are another thing entirely."

"You must have a few ideas," Mel prodded. "Was Henry openly fighting with anyone before his death?"

"He was openly fighting with everyone. He cheated at cards."

"Yes, but cheating at cards isn't a capital punishment offense," Mel argued. "Whoever killed him must've had motive."

"Wait." Annie furrowed her brow. "Are you saying someone really killed him?"

"I'm saying his death wasn't due to natural causes like we originally thought," Mel replied. "It seems that Henry was murdered ... and we're going to find out who did it."

"Huh." Annie rubbed her cheek, her expression thoughtful. "I thought Harper and Zander were asking questions because they were bored and Henry was a neighbor. I didn't think they were really on to anything."

"Yes, well, I was hopeful that was the case," Jared said. "It appears that they were right, though."

"I still think you should keep that to yourself," Mel warned. "If you admit she was right, you'll never hear the end of it. I'm married. I know."

"He's definitely right," Carl said. "Women are unbearable when they think they're right."

"We're sunshine and daisies whether we're right or wrong," Annie argued. "Get over yourself."

"Whatever." Carl rolled his eyes. "I'm sick of women. The whole lot of you are crazy."

"I hear that." Glenn brandished his thumb again. "I think she broke it."

Jared scowled. "You're fine. You learned a valuable lesson about keeping your hands to yourself."

"All I heard was blah, blah, blah."

Mel tugged on his limited patience. "All we want to know is who Henry spent his time with when he was here, Annie. We don't want to take up too much of your precious time."

"He hopped around," Annie answered. "He never stayed with one group for more than one day because he irritated everyone. He spent all his time boasting about the tickets he used to give and annoying people. No one purposely wanted to spend time with him."

"That's not entirely true," Eve hedged. "One person did visit with him on a regular basis."

Jared leaned forward, interested. "Who?"

"His granddaughter. She went out of her way to see him at least two or three times a week."

That was news to Jared. "Do you happen to know why?"

Eve shrugged. "I think she was something of a suck-up."

Glenn enthusiastically nodded, his injured thumb forgotten. "You've got that right. In my day, kids that age didn't pretend to be interested, they were either really interested or they got smacked around. Geez, I really miss the old days."

"Yeah, I can totally see that," Jared said dryly.

MARLEY DIDN'T LOOK HAPPY TO SEE ZANDER AND HARPER approaching.

"Oh, man. What do you want?"

Mike, his hand planted on Marley's rear end, snickered. "I think they're members of your fan club or something."

"I think so, too," Marley said, rolling her eyes. "We're not doing nothing."

"Anything," Harper automatically corrected, instantly wishing she could go back in time and refrain from doing such a good impression of her mother. "Of course, if you want to say 'nothing,' that's completely up to you."

Zander chuckled. "Nice save."

"Thank you."

Marley made an exaggerated face. "Well, that's thirty seconds of my life I'll never get back. Is there something you guys want?"

Harper bit back a hot retort and kept her expression neutral even though she wanted to give Marley a good hair yank to see if the girl could make anything other than an agitating expression. "I just wanted to see how you were doing. I stopped in at your house and spent some time with your mother this morning."

Marley's eyes sparked with interest. "Why would you do that?"

"Because your mother is in mourning."

"My mother didn't like my grandfather any more than I did. She's happy he's gone."

The look on Marley's face was like a punch in the gut for Harper. She'd never met a more hateful child. It had to be an act. That's what Harper kept telling herself, at least. There could be no other explanation for the girl's churlish ways.

"You don't have to act this way." Harper lowered her voice. "You don't have to impress this guy. It's okay to be upset about your grandfather's passing. In fact, it's normal to be upset over something like that."

"Who says I'm normal?"

"Hey, I'm the king of being abnormal," Zander interjected, ignoring the amused look on Mike's face. "Losing a grandparent is still a big deal. It's okay to be upset."

"I'm not upset," Marley insisted. "He wasn't a very nice guy and he always picked on me. If he wanted me to be upset, he should've been nicer."

"He was still your grandfather," Harper pressed.

"That doesn't mean I care about him dying." Marley cast a quick look to Mike. "These guys are boring me. Do you want to head over to the ice cream shop?"

Mike nodded without hesitation. "You can buy me a cone."

"Why do I have to buy?" Marley didn't so much as glance back at Harper and Zander as she moved away from them. She'd essentially dismissed them and wasn't interested in their offered words of comfort or disdain.

"Because you promised to buy me something with your inheritance and that's not going to happen for weeks. I need something to keep my interest now."

Harper's mouth dropped open as she swiveled to face Zander. "Did you hear that?"

"Yeah. She's a complete and total terror. I think she's definitely capable of killing her grandfather."

Harper lightly slapped Zander's arm. "Not that. The part where Mike said she promised to buy him something with her inheritance and that's the only reason he's hanging around."

"Oh. I guess I wasn't really listening." Zander cocked his head to the side, considering. "They're both world-class jerkwads. I don't see why we're wasting our time talking to either of them."

Harper's expression was incredulous. "Seriously? That's what you got out of that conversation?"

"What was I supposed to get out of that conversation?"

"Marley is bribing her boyfriend with gifts to stay with her."

"So? Lots of people enjoy a good bribe. I happen to be one of them. Shawn doesn't bribe me, but I might like him more if he did."

Harper didn't believe that, but she wasn't in the mood for another relationship argument. "Yes, but you said Mike was a big deal because he's quarterback of the football team."

"I did say that. So?"

"So what if Marley is desperate to find ways to hold on to him?"

Realization finally dawned on Zander's face. "Oh. You think she killed her grandfather for the inheritance. That's what you're saying, right?"

Harper rolled the notion through her head. She wasn't sure if she really believed that. She couldn't fully discount it either, though. "I think it's a possibility."

"So ... what's the plan?"

"We need to follow those kids and learn more about their relationship."

Zander let loose with a long-suffering sigh. "Fine. But I'm going to need more coffee if you expect me to do that." He turned and made to follow but Harper stilled him with a hand on his arm.

"Not now. We have to wait until after dark. We don't want them to see us doing it."

"Oh." Zander wrinkled his nose. "Does that mean we're going on a covert operation tonight?"

Harper nodded. "Just you and me. Shawn and Jared won't understand."

Zander brightened. "It will be just like old times."

Harper matched his smile. "Exactly."

"Yay!"

"And you thought I could get bored of you." Harper made a clucking sound with her tongue. "You're the only person who likes covert operations as much as me. I could never get bored with you."

"I know. I was being silly."

"You definitely were."

ELEVEN

"Wait ... so he was poisoned?"

Zander stood next to the stove shortly before dinner, tongs in hand, and fixed Jared with an unreadable expression.

"He was poisoned," Jared confirmed, sipping his Coke and keeping his eyes forward rather than risk a look toward Harper. He was terrified what he would find there. Options included tears, anger, and haughty happiness. He wasn't sure which he preferred at this point.

"What kind of poison?" Shawn asked. He either didn't notice the tension or opted to ignore it. Jared was thankful for that.

"Arsenic."

"Oh, that's old school," Zander noted. "That's something straight out of a mystery from the seventies. In fact, I'm pretty sure that the mother used arsenic in *Flowers in the Attic*. That's definitely old school."

Shawn furrowed his brow. "Isn't that the book where the brother and sister are locked in an attic for years and get it on?"

Zander nodded. "My mother had it. She told me not to read it, which meant I had no choice but to read it. The entire thing was very ... um ... disturbing."

"You loved that book," Harper argued, her voice close enough to

Jared's ear to cause him to jolt. "You made me read it and then comment on the sex scenes because you were convinced there was some undercurrent in the book that you didn't understand."

"Those sex scenes were tasteful."

"It was still incest."

"Tasteful incest."

"Oh, whatever."

Jared tapped his thumb on the kitchen table, unsure how to proceed. "How did the conversation turn to incest?"

"Zander is here," Shawn answered simply. "What happens now with the case? How do you track down the murderer?"

"We're still conducting interviews." Jared finally geared up the courage to glance at Harper and found her expression flat. "We have to figure out how the arsenic got into the house and exactly how Henry ingested it. We didn't find anything when we were over there this afternoon so the state police tech team is coming in to test."

"Arsenic isn't easily available, is it?" Harper asked.

"Not really. It's naturally occurring in some places, but I can guarantee none of those places are in Henry Spencer's house."

"Hmm." Harper rubbed her finger over her lip. "It's a lot to take in."

"It is," Jared agreed, shifting on his chair. The fact that Harper refused to crow about being right set his teeth on edge. He wanted to get the conversation out in the open so they could move past it. "I suppose you want to give me a good 'I told you so,' huh?"

Harper was evasive. "Why would I want to do that?"

"Because you've earned it."

"Well ... ." Harper broke off and glanced to Zander. "I think I'm above that. I don't need to be right to feel good about myself."

"Oh, whatever." Zander offered up an exasperated expression. "We both know you want to sing ... or dance ... or maybe a combination of both. Quite frankly, I think you should do it. He called you a liar, Harp. Let him have it."

Jared balked. "I did not call her a liar."

"You didn't believe her when she said it was possibly murder," Zander argued. "You had zero faith in her investigative abilities."

"Yeah, well, speaking of that ... ."

Harper cut off Jared. "I don't need to be right. I'm simply glad the truth is out there and now we can move forward and find the correct answers."

"There is no *we* moving forward," Jared cautioned. "This is a police investigation. You guys have no standing in it."

Harper narrowed her eyes. "Excuse me?"

"Heart, don't look at me that way," Jared grumbled. "You're not an investigator."

"I am an investigator," Harper shot back. "I investigate things all the time."

"Ghosts."

"And Henry is a ghost."

"Yes, but Henry is a ghost who is confused about what happened." Jared chose his words carefully. "He doesn't know who killed him. He thinks assassins are after him. He was liked by almost no one and loved by few. I don't think Henry can help with this investigation."

"Which means I can't help," Harper surmised, her heart twisting. "Wow. Just ... wow."

Harper pressed her hands to the table as she stood.

"Where are you going?" Jared asked, worry overtaking him. "You're not going to storm out, are you?"

"I'm an adult. I don't storm out."

Jared was relieved and yet the look in Harper's eyes gave him pause. "So ... what are you doing?"

"Going outside to work on the cemetery."

"How is that different from storming out?"

"I won't lock you out of the bedroom and make you sleep on the couch," Harper replied, her tone biting. "I have work to do."

"Dinner will be ready in twenty minutes," Zander called out.

"Great. I can't wait."

Jared heaved out a sigh, his shoulders hopping when Harper slammed the front door with enough force to shake the walls. He waited a beat, sipped his soda, and then fixed his full attention on Zander. "This is all your fault. You know that, right?"

Zander refused to engage in a ludicrous debate. "Blaming me isn't going to fix this situation."

"And what is going to fix this situation?"

"A little faith might help."

"Ugh." Jared lowered his forehead to his palm. "Do you really believe I don't have faith in her?"

"I don't know. I know she's been twisting herself with worry for a week because of you – something I told her she was ludicrous to believe in the first place – and her reward for trying to move on is apparently an invisible smack across the face."

Jared was dumbfounded. "Why is she worried?"

"Because she thinks you're going to grow so sick of me that you'll toss her over eventually." Zander saw no reason to lie. Sure, Harper confided in him under a veil of secrecy, but everyone knew he couldn't keep his mouth shut so he couldn't be blamed for being a gossip. "I told her you loved her and she was being ridiculous, but she can't help herself from worrying sometimes."

"I do love her," Jared supplied. "I'm not going to toss her over no matter how irritated I get with you. How can she think that?"

Zander shrugged. "She's never had a boyfriend like you ... one who managed to stick around so long."

"She was with Quinn a long time," Jared pointed out, referring to Harper's former boyfriend. He went out for a drive one day years before, was involved in some sort of accident, wandered away from the vehicle while injured and was presumed dead in the woods surrounding Whisper Cove. The accident traumatized Harper, and Jared was well aware he shouldn't push her on the details even though he was beyond curious. "Why am I different from him?"

"Because she didn't love Quinn."

However ridiculous, hearing the words made Jared feel better. He had nothing against a dead man, but he didn't want the memory of Quinn Jackson hanging over his future with Harper. "That still doesn't explain why she's so worked up."

"Oh, you're such a ninny."

Shawn made a quelling sound to dissuade Zander from continuing, a noise Zander pretended he didn't hear.

"She's never gotten to this point in a relationship," Zander explained. "Heck, neither of us have. I'm much more adaptable and easygoing than she is, though."

Shawn and Jared exchanged dubious looks.

"So why is she worried?" Jared pressed. "Does she doubt that I love her?"

"No. She knows you love her. We're coming up to an important crossroad, though. She doesn't know how to handle it."

"And what crossroad is that?"

"The one where eventually we're going to have to think about separating into two households."

Jared couldn't swallow his gasp in time to keep Zander from hearing it. "You've been talking about that?"

"Oh, look at you. You're so relieved it makes me want to punch you in the ... well, you know where. Of course we've been talking about it. Life is about to change. We always talk about big life changes."

"And what is she saying?"

"She says that she's worried I'm going to melt down when it comes time to switch things up. She says that she'll always love me and we will still spend time together so I shouldn't cry or anything."

It took everything Jared had not to explode at Zander. "I meant about me. What is she saying about me?"

"Oh, why does everything have to be about you? Sometimes things are about me."

"Yes, more often than not, things are about you," Jared gritted out. "I want to focus on me, though. Is she open to us getting our own place?"

Jared's reaction caused Zander to change tactics. "Have you been considering getting a place for just the two of you? I'm going to be honest, I didn't think you were there yet. I thought we had a little time."

"I don't want to rush her," Jared clarified. "That's the last thing I want. A little privacy would be good for all of us, though. Shawn and I have been talking ... ."

Zander held up his tongs to cut off Jared. "You two have been talking behind our backs?"

"Thanks, man," Shawn interjected, rubbing the back of his neck. "I appreciate you sharing that."

"I'm sorry." Jared meant it. "It's no different for Shawn and me to talk than it is for you and Harper to talk. That only seems fair."

"It doesn't sound remotely fair to me, but I'm going to let that go ... for now," Zander said. "What is it exactly that you have planned?"

"I haven't gotten that far," Jared replied, his eyes flashing. "I was too afraid to bring it up with her because I thought she would dismiss the idea outright. If that happens ... ."

Instead of thinking about himself for a change, Zander looked at things from Jared's point of view and felt a swell of sympathy. "You were afraid that she would say no and then you guys would lose whatever momentum you have in your relationship."

"Yeah, I guess that's exactly how I feel."

"That's not going to happen."

"How can you be sure?"

"Because she loves you and knows that eventually you guys are going to move out on your own," Zander replied without hesitation. "She's not an idiot. She knows we can't live together forever even though I've given her several ways that will work."

"Just out of curiosity, how do you see that working?" Shawn asked.

"I was thinking a huge house where all four of us could spread out ... or maybe adjacent townhouses ... or maybe a duplex."

"All of those are fun ideas, but you love this house," Jared said. "Plus, I don't think that gives us enough space. I want her close to you but not on top of you."

"I know that." Zander kept his voice even. "That's one of the reasons I like you. Most men wouldn't put up with my friendship with Harper. In fact, do you think Quinn let me climb into bed with them every morning?"

"I would rather not think about Harper sharing a bed with him." Jared's smile was rueful. "It's petty and jealous, but I can't help it."

"Don't worry about Quinn. Harper cares more about you than she ever did for Quinn. The only hold he has over her is the fact that they never found his body. If they had, she would've let go a long time ago. She's still convinced his ghost is out there roaming ... alone. That's what she can't let go. She and Quinn never would've made it if he survived."

"You've told me that before, but it's nice to hear," Jared said. "Still, I want to give Harper what she needs. What does she want?"

"You to believe in her."

Jared balked. "I *do* believe in her."

"Do you? It sounds to me as if you don't. Even though she was right about Henry being murdered, you came in here and told her she couldn't be involved. How do you think that makes her feel?"

"I don't know. I want her safe. There's a murderer running around out there and I don't want Harper to be next on his or her list ... especially since she's still getting over what happened at the asylum."

"She won't talk about that and you need to give her space," Zander said. "When she's ready, she'll open up. For now she's still absorbing things. You can't force her to move faster."

"So what should I do right now to make her feel better?"

"I think you already know the answer to that."

Jared stared at him for a long beat. "You're right. I do."

JARED FOUND HARPER FUSSING WITH THE MAKESHIFT cemetery. She wore a hoodie and her cheeks were pink from the cold. She didn't look in his direction when he stepped on the porch and Jared knew she was angry. That didn't stop him from approaching.

"You know I love you, right?"

As far as openings go, Harper had heard worse. "I love you, too."

"I don't want to fight."

"Then don't tell me what to do."

"That's not really how I look at it." Jared shuffled closer to Harper and grabbed one side of a fake tombstone so he could help her line it up. "I don't want to order you around. That's not what I'm about. I hope you know that."

Harper lifted her eyes. "What are you about?"

"Protecting you."

"I'm not in danger. How is it you think I'm in danger?"

"I don't know, Heart, but the idea of you going after a murderer doesn't fill me with visions of unicorns and dancing bears."

Harper wrinkled her forehead. "I don't even know what that means."

"I worry about you." Jared decided honesty was the best policy and told the truth. "I admire you. I think you're talented. The things you do are amazing. That doesn't mean I can just sit back and let you do something crazy."

"What makes you think I'm going to do something crazy?"

Jared smirked. "I've met you. Sometimes you can't help yourself."

"I'm not going to do anything crazy." Harper snagged Jared's coat sleeve. "I promise. I just want to help Henry."

"You always want to help. Your heart is so big that you can't help yourself from diving in and helping before you've considered the ramifications of what might happen."

"And what might happen?"

"Well, for starters, Henry was poisoned."

"I know. He was murdered. I believe I'm the one who told you that."

Jared bit the inside of his cheek to keep from laughing. "I thought you weren't going to say 'I told you so.'"

"I forgot."

"That's okay. You've earned it. I gave Mel a big, fat 'I told you so' on your behalf when I heard."

Harper visibly brightened. "You did?"

"I did. I was happy for you that you were right."

"Cool."

"I was unhappy for myself, though, because I knew that meant you would get even more involved in this case," Jared said. "Heart, I can't stop myself from fearing that one day you'll stumble across a body and get into more trouble than you can get yourself out of. I can't help it. I worry."

"I think that's fair." Harper adopted a pragmatic tone. "The thing is, I worry about you, too. You're a police officer. You could go down in the line of duty because that's part of your job description."

Jared balked. "I can't change who I am."

"I can't either. The difference is, I accept that about you. You don't seem to be able to do the same for me."

Jared opened his mouth to argue and then snapped it shut as he considered the statement. "You're right."

Harper was ready to push her argument further until he stunned her with the two simple words. "I'm right?"

"You are. You were a fully formed adult before I came into your life. I loved you anyway. I fell in love with you because of who you are. I can't expect you to change. In truth, I don't want you to change."

"So why are we arguing?"

Jared held his hands palms out. "I have no idea, but I want it to stop."

Harper stepped forward and slid her arms around Jared's neck, giving him a tight hug. "I'm glad you don't want me to change."

Jared chuckled as he appreciatively rubbed her back. "I'm glad you don't want me to change."

"Does that mean I can help you on the case?"

"No."

Harper's smile slipped. "I knew you were going to say that."

"I love you the way you are, but I'm not going to encourage you to find danger. I can't do that. I'm sorry."

Harper was earnest. "I can't back away from this. I have to know what happened to Henry."

"I guess that's fair. I can't get behind you being reckless, though."

"I promise not to be reckless."

"Good." Jared pressed a kiss to her mouth. "So ... fight over?"

Harper nodded. "Let's go inside. I'm starving."

"That sounds like a plan." Jared gave her another kiss. "I thought, over dinner, you could tell me what you were doing at Carol's house and the senior center. How does that sound?"

Harper scowled. "Like I'm going to be in trouble when I'm done."

"Well, at least we'll have fun making up twice in the same day."

"That's something to look forward to, huh?"

TWELVE

"We have to run to the office."

Harper and Zander were the picture of innocence when they appeared in the living room about an hour after dinner.

Jared sat on the couch with Shawn, a baseball game on the television, and suspiciously looked them up and down. They wore the same clothes from before, nothing had physically changed, and yet he was convinced they were up to something. "Why?"

"Because we need to check messages and emails," Zander replied perfunctorily. "We haven't been in the office for a bit and they're probably piling up."

"Can't you do that from here?"

"We can, but we need to go over the books, too. They're at the office."

Yeah. Jared was convinced they were up to something now. They sounded rehearsed. "I thought your accounting software was on the computer?"

"The *office* computer."

"Yes, but you back it up in the cloud," Jared noted. "I know because you've sung songs about how much you love the cloud."

"We also want to pick up some pumpkin ice cream from downtown as a special snack," Harper added. "We won't be gone long."

Jared ran his tongue over his teeth, considering. "I can come with you." He made to stand.

"Oh, you don't need to come with us," Harper said hurriedly. "You're comfortable ... and watching the game."

"Yes, but I can carry the ice cream."

"I think we can manage." Harper's smile never wavered, but Jared sensed annoyance positively rolling off her diminutive shoulders.

Rather than push the issue, Jared returned to his reclining position. "Okay. Have fun."

Harper couldn't hide her surprise. "That's it?"

"Should I argue further?"

"No. We won't be gone long."

"Okay. Make sure that you're not."

Jared remained sitting for a full minute once Harper closed the door before getting to his feet and wandering to the front window.

"What are you doing?" Shawn asked, curious.

"Just checking something." Jared hid behind the curtains and peered through the small opening near the wall so he could see through the window without detection, his mouth tipping down into a scowl after less than thirty seconds of spying.

"What do you see?"

"I knew they were lying."

"What are they doing?"

"They're changing their clothes."

"Outside? It's cold out."

"Yes, but they didn't want to tip me off ... the little sneaks." Jared made a disgusted sound in the back of his throat. "I'm going to yell like you wouldn't believe when they get back."

"Get back?" Shawn had trouble following Jared's train of thought. "Where are they going?"

"I have no idea, but we're going to follow them."

"We are?"

"Yup."

"But ... it's the baseball playoffs." Shawn didn't look happy with their change of plans. "What could they possibly be doing that's so terrible?"

"Why do you think I'm following them?"

"I CAN'T BELIEVE HE FELL FOR THAT."

Zander was practically crowing in the passenger seat of Harper's car as his best friend focused on the road.

"He didn't fall for that," Harper scoffed. "He knew we were lying."

"Bull. I'm an expert liar. He had no idea."

"Please. He's not an idiot. He knew."

"If he knew, why didn't he call us on it?" Zander challenged.

"Because he's waiting for us to get back so he can nail us on our home turf. By the way, don't let me forget that pumpkin ice cream."

"If he already knows we're lying, why do we need the ice cream?"

"Because, if we're going to fight, I want a good dessert to bolster my spirits after."

"Oh. Good plan." Zander stretched out his long legs in front of him. "So how do you know where Marley is going to be tonight? You heard the same thing I did. They didn't say where they were going."

"No, but it's October in Whisper Cove. They don't have a lot of options."

"So ... where are they going?"

"Where did we go when we were their age?"

"The parking lot of the grocery store."

"Where else?"

"The cemetery."

"Ding, ding, ding. We have a winner!"

"Huh. I guess that makes sense." Zander rolled his shoulders. "Do you think the kids still hang out by the mausoleum?"

"I know they do. I stumbled across them four times last October. They didn't seem bothered that I knew what they were doing and even invited me for a beer."

"Did you take them up on it?"

"Of course not."

"Did you only not take them up on it because you were afraid the cops would show up and arrest you for aiding the delinquency of a minor?"

Harper sighed. "Maybe a little."

"You're such a prude."

"Yeah, yeah, yeah."

"WHERE DO YOU THINK THEY'RE GOING?"

Despite his earlier reticence, Shawn seemed to be enjoying the game as he sat in Jared's truck and watched the police officer navigate traffic in an effort to follow Harper and Zander.

"It looks as if they're going to the cemetery, although I have no idea why."

"Maybe they're looking for Henry's ghost," Shawn suggested.

"I guess that's a possibility." Jared ran the idea through his head. "I don't see why they would do that, though. Henry has visited twice, both times at the house. He's not buried in the cemetery yet. He's still at the mortuary."

"Are you sure?"

Jared nodded. "We visited with his daughter this morning. His funeral isn't for another three days. Apparently he had very specific demands and the coffin pillow is backordered."

"Oh, well, maybe they're doing something else."

"Like what?"

"I don't know." Shawn shrugged. "They hunt ghosts for a living. Maybe they got an emergency call."

"And why would they keep that to themselves? It's hardly something to lie over."

"I'm not sure." Shawn tapped his chin. "Maybe they're meeting someone and don't want us to know. In fact, maybe they're both having affairs and are using each other as alibis. Crap. Do you think that's it?"

Jared let loose with a long-suffering sigh. "I think you spend too much time with Zander. He's starting to be a bad influence on you."

"Fine. If you don't think they're having affairs, what are they doing?"

"I don't know. I know I don't like it, though."

HARPER AND ZANDER PARKED AT THE BACK OF THE cemetery, leaving Harper's car near the ditch and not so much as looking over their shoulders before creeping onto the property. Had they bothered to look, they would've seen Jared's truck ... and known they were in a boatload of trouble.

Instead they stuck to the tree line that skirted the edge of the property and picked their way toward the mausoleum, which was the only landmark that stuck out in the area.

"I see movement," Zander whispered, gripping Harper's hand as they tromped through the underbrush. "I think you were right about kids being out here. We don't know that it's our kids, though."

"We don't, but it won't be hard to find out."

They made the rest of the trip in absolute silence, crouching low beneath a pine tree and watching a handful of figures cavort in front of the building. One of those figures just happened to be a blond – like Marley – and doing cartwheels in front of the building.

"She's not very broken up, is she?" Zander made a face. "Wait ... what are they doing? That doesn't look like a beer keg."

Harper managed to drag her derisive stare from Marley and focus on the pile of items sitting on the lawn. It was hard to make out exactly what was there, but after a moment of studied concentration Harper realized what the biggest item was.

"It's a case of toilet paper."

Zander was taken aback. "In case they really have to go?"

Harper made a face. "No." She pressed her finger to her lips. "It's windy, but they still might hear us. Keep your voice low."

"Hey, I'm not doing anything wrong," Zander reminded her. "If I want to talk, I'll talk. However, since I'm curious, why would they need a case of toilet paper if they weren't worried about ... you know, hygiene?"

Harper had to fight the urge to smack her best friend upside the head. "Think about it, Zander. It's October in Whisper Cove. What else do you use toilet paper for?"

"To blot lipstick."

"What else?"

"To stuff bras." Zander took a long look at Marley. "She doesn't need toilet paper like you did."

Harper was affronted. "I didn't need toilet paper. I was perfectly happy with my body."

"You stuffed and we both know it. Who are you trying to kid?"

"I did not stuff."

"You did so."

"I did not."

"You did ... ."

They both broke off at the sound of a twig snapping, swiveling at the same time and widening their eyes to comical proportions when they realized Shawn and Jared stood in the shadows watching them.

"Uh-oh."

Zander was less succinct. "Do you think they'll chase us if we run?"

"What good will that do?" Harper was annoyed. "They already know we lied and what we're doing."

"Oh, we know you lied," Jared corrected. "I'm still unsure what you're doing."

Harper scratched her cheek with a gloved hand and then pointed. "We ran into Marley again this afternoon. We're spying on her because she's acting weird."

"I see." Jared's demeanor was hard to read. "And how did you know she would be here?"

"This is where the kids hang out in the fall. There aren't a lot of options in Whisper Cove."

"Uh-huh." Jared rolled his neck until it cracked. "And what did Marley say that set you off?"

Harper had no choice so she repeated the conversation she over-heard. When she was done, she braced herself for Jared to start yelling.

"That *does* sound odd," he conceded, crouching as he moved closer in an effort to get a better view. His eyes were impassive as he watched the girl cartwheel across the lawn. "Do you really think she's a murderer?"

"I really think she's an unkind and entitled girl. She won't stop talking about the money her grandfather is supposedly leaving to her and she's paying that boy to date her."

"Just for the record, I happen to be one of those people who isn't above a bribe," Zander offered helpfully to Shawn.

"Good to know," Shawn said dryly. "I don't understand why you lied. Why not tell the truth?"

"I wanted to tell the truth," Zander replied. "Harper said no because Jared thinks he's a babysitter rather than a supportive boyfriend."

Jared balked. "I think nothing of the sort."

"That's not what Harper said."

Jared held up a hand to silence him. "That's not what I said, Heart. Why would you tell him something like that?"

"That's what I heard."

"Then we need to buy Q-tips on the way home so you can clean your ears," Jared grumbled. "I'm really mad about you lying, by the way. We're going to have a long talk about it when we get home."

"Are we going to make up when we're done fighting?"

"Only if you have that pumpkin ice cream you got me geeked about."

Harper's lips curved. "Deal."

Jared gave her a quick kiss. "We're still going to talk about this. Lying is not okay."

"I know. It's just ... I didn't want to turn it into a big thing."

"Good job. I ... ." Jared broke off when he realized the noise next to the mausoleum had ceased. When he lifted his head, he found ten teenagers staring in their direction. They didn't look happy. "Well, crap. I need to handle this."

Harper nodded knowingly. "They have toilet paper. I think they're your prankster vandals."

"Ah. Good catch. That's a much better reason to be out here than I was going to give them."

"And what was that?"

"Overactive adult hormones. I was hoping that would be enough for them to think we're 'icky' and start running."

"Hmm. Either one would've worked."

"True."

MEL WAS ABSOLUTELY FURIOUS WHEN HE ARRIVED ON the scene. The teenagers wisely opted not to flee when they caught sight of Jared – mostly because Harper and Zander recognized them so there was no point – but they were in foul moods when Mel popped into view.

"What is going on?"

"I believe I found our pranksters," Jared explained, keeping his gaze on Mike because he believed the boy showed signs of running.

"What makes you say that?"

Jared pointed at the mountain of items on the ground. "Toilet paper. Shaving cream. Condoms. What else do you think that's for?"

"Maybe they're having some sort of freaky mating ritual," Mel replied. "Did you ever think of that?"

"What about the eggs?"

"Maybe it was freaky deaky or something." Mel said the words, but he eyed the teenagers with overt disdain all the same. "Are you guys responsible for the recent spate of vandalism?"

"We have no idea what you're talking about," Marley replied, adopting an air of practiced innocence. "We were just walking by when that guy jumped out of the bushes and frightened us. We were minding our own business and then ... there he was." She leaned closer to Mel and finished in a conspiratorial whisper. "I think he's a pervert or something."

"Uh-huh." Mel wasn't convinced. "You were just walking by and happened to stumble across a mountain of toilet paper, did you?"

"We didn't put it here."

"Yeah. Go stand over there and keep your mouth shut for a moment. I need to talk to my partner."

"Whatever you say, Detective Kelsey. I respect you because you're the most admired member of our law enforcement team."

Mel smiled as he smoothed his uniform. "Thank you."

"You're welcome."

"I'm not an idiot who is going to fall for that, though."

Marley's smile slipped. "I was telling the truth."

"Well, now you're being quiet." Mel shuffled closer to Jared, sparing a glance for Zander, Harper, and Shawn as he made a clucking sound with his tongue. "What going on here?"

Jared shrugged, seemingly unbothered. "Do you want the truth or a lie?"

"Which one is better."

"They're both equally good stories."

Mel heaved out a sigh. "Fine. Give me the truth."

Jared launched into the tale. When he was done, the look on Mel's face was comical. "So, as you can see, it started out as juvenile spying and turned into the capture of a criminal team."

"Criminal team?" Mel rolled his eyes. "They're kids with toilet paper and eggs. That's normal for this time of year."

"Yes, well, that's our story and we're sticking to it."

Mel dragged a frustrated hand through his hair. "I don't even know what to say about this." His eyes narrowed when he focused on Zander. "I suppose this is your fault, huh?"

Zander was having none of it. "Oh, right. Like I'm the one who likes crawling around in the woods after dark. I think you should move your gaze toward something blond and leave me out of it."

Mel focused on Harper. "And you did this because you think Marley might've killed her grandfather for her inheritance?"

"Well, when you say it like that, it sounds stupid," Harper hedged. "I know what I saw and heard, though. She's acting weird. I don't know how to explain it."

Mel glanced over his shoulder and watched Marley for a moment. Despite the fact that the police were on the scene, she seemed much more interested in Mike than her predicament.

"I can see that," he said after a beat. "There's just one problem; I got a copy of Henry's will toward the end of shift. I was looking through it when I got the call."

Marley, who was fixated on Mike only moments before, focused on Mel. Her interest was evident.

"Henry Spencer's will was filled out twenty years ago," Mel continued. "That's long before Marley was born. It hasn't been changed in that time."

"Which means she's not in the will," Jared mused.

"No."

"What?" Marley was incensed as she stomped forward, hands on hips. "That can't be right. My grandfather told me he was going to leave me something special. He promised."

"Unless that something special comes in the form of a letter from the grave, you're fresh out," Mel fired back. "You're not in the will. I checked with his estate lawyer to be sure there wasn't a mistake, but he said the will stands. You, my dear, are not a beneficiary."

Marley let loose with a frustrated shriek. "If he wasn't already dead I would kill him myself!"

Harper and Jared exchanged a quick look, Harper turning sheepish under his challenging stare.

"Huh. Well ... now what?"

"Now you buy some ice cream and we go home to fight," Jared replied, not missing a beat.

"What about your criminals?" Mel asked.

"I figured you would want to handle them."

Mel scowled. "You're real piece of work. Has anyone ever told you that?"

Jared shrugged. "Thanks, partner. I'll see you tomorrow morning. I'm really looking forward to it."

Mel's expression was dark. "So am I. You have no idea."

❧ 13 ❧

THIRTEEN

"**A**re you going to get in trouble because of me?" Harper blurted out the question with little finesse.

Jared stood in front of his truck shortly before ten and watched Shawn and Zander make their way into the house. The excursion to the cemetery lasted much longer than he expected and he was thankful Mel ultimately capitulated and agreed to handle the paperwork on his own. Otherwise Jared would still be at the department and that was the last thing he wanted. When he shifted his eyes to Harper, he found her staring at him with wide-eyed wonder.

"Why would I get in trouble?"

"Because you were technically spying on teenagers."

"Yes, that's a lovely way to look at it."

Harper clasped her hands together, nervous energy threatening to overtake her. "It could get out that you're creepy and hang around the woods."

"Thankfully I wasn't alone. When the gossip mill hits, we'll be creepy together."

"I'm already creepy as far as most of the people in town are concerned," Harper pointed out. "My reputation can't really take a hit in their eyes. You, on the other hand, are shiny and new and could fall in their estimation."

Jared stared at her for a long beat. "I've been here since the spring. That's six months. I'm hardly new."

"Most of the people in Whisper Cove are lifers. You'll always be the newbie."

"Good to know." Jared slipped a strand of hair behind Harper's ear. "For the record, I don't care what the townsfolk think of me. I care what you think of me."

"I happen to love you."

"That was a good answer. That doesn't negate the fact that you lied."

"I know." Harper hung her head in shame so pronounced Jared had to bite the inside of his cheek to keep from laughing.

He managed to keep a straight face ... but just barely. "Can you tell me why you lied?"

"I didn't know what else to do."

"That's not much of an answer."

"That's because very little thought went into making the decision," Harper supplied, crossing her arms as she leaned against the front of Jared's truck. "I don't know why I lied. I guess it was because I knew you would fight me if you knew the truth."

"Yes, but did you really think I would believe the lie you spun?"

"Obviously not."

"Heart, you knew I wouldn't believe that lie even when you were telling it," Jared argued. "I saw it on your face when you were doing it. You knew. So why did you do it?"

"Honestly? I thought you would stay here and stew about it and we wouldn't have to fight until I got back. I knew we would fight, but I thought the ice cream would soften things and it would be okay."

"Speaking of that, where is the ice cream?" Jared lifted his head and studied Harper's empty hands.

"Zander has it."

"Is there enough for everyone or do I need to wrestle him for it?"

Harper cracked a smile, but it was small and tremulous. "I'm sorry I lied."

"I am, too." Jared turned serious. "I was hoping we were building a relationship free of lies."

Harper balked. "It wasn't a big lie."

"It was a lie that could've got you into trouble."

"How? Those kids had toilet paper and eggs. I think I would've survived."

"And what if there was someone else hanging out there besides the kids ... like a murderer, for example?"

"Um ... ." Harper pressed her lips together as she considered the question. "I didn't really think about that."

"I know. I figured that out on my own."

"I wasn't trying to lie," Harper pressed. "Okay, I mean, I *was* trying to lie. It wasn't a big lie, though. I wouldn't lie about the big stuff."

Jared remained calm even though part of him wanted to yell and the other part wanted to laugh. "This relationship stuff is only going to work if we tell each other the truth. I'm not a stickler for absolute honesty or anything – like I don't care if you and Zander gossip about things and then lie and say you weren't gossiping – but the big stuff needs to be true."

"Yeah." Harper absently scratched her cheek. "And, just for the record, you think that following kids in a cemetery is big stuff, right?"

"I think that taking off after dark when there's a murderer on the loose is big stuff," Jared clarified. "Had you told me that you were planning on following teenagers, I probably wouldn't have gotten so worked up about the situation. Although, to be fair, I still would've gone with you."

"Because you like to be overbearing?"

Jared scowled. "Because I love you enough to want to protect you forever. I believe that's allowed."

"It is. I was just checking." Harper stared at him for a long beat before sneaking her index finger out and snagging it on his pinkie.

Jared didn't want to be charmed – he was angry with her, he reminded himself – but he couldn't stop his lips from twitching. He considered bringing up the things Zander mentioned earlier – he was eager to talk about a possible change in their living situation, after all – but he knew now wasn't the time. That conversation would have to wait until the case was over ... or at least until he wasn't trying to pretend they were having a serious conversation.

"Harper, I love you very much." Jared forced himself to be serious. "While I wouldn't have been happy about you and Zander taking off into the night to stalk a bunch of high schoolers, I would much prefer knowing about it from the beginning rather than having to follow you to find out the truth."

Harper was sheepish. "For the record, I was going to tell you what we were doing when I got back."

"That's very sweet." Jared ran his free hand through his hair. "I want you to feel comfortable telling me about your adventures before they happen."

Harper balked. "You want me to admit I'm doing something illegal to a cop?"

"What did you do that was illegal?"

"I stalked underage kids."

"Oh, well, that." Jared's smile was rueful. "I still want to know."

"And do you promise you won't bust me if I tell you before I do it?"

"No."

"Then how does that work out in my favor?"

Jared shrugged as he took a step closer and slipped his arms around her waist. "I promise to love you no matter what. That's the best I can do."

Harper heaved out a sigh. "Fine. I guess I'm going to simply have to trust you to keep your promise."

"It's a promise I want to keep so that shouldn't be too hard."

"Yeah, yeah, yeah." Harper pressed a kiss to the corner of his mouth. "What do you think Mel is going to say tomorrow morning when you get to work?"

Jared's smile slipped. "Nothing good."

"Yeah. I don't think so either."

"OKAY, EVEN THOUGH THE NIGHT DIDN'T GO EXACTLY HOW I thought it would, I have to say this ice cream is worth the crap I'm going to have to put up with tomorrow." Jared twirled his spoon and licked the orange treat with a flourish. "How come we've never had this ice cream before?"

"Because they only do the pumpkin flavored stuff in October. We'll eat it all month, though, so take heart."

"Definitely." Jared kissed Harper's forehead when she rested it against his shoulder, scraped his spoon across the bottom of his container a final time, and then turned serious. "Do you still think Marley killed her grandfather?"

The shift in the conversation caught Harper off guard. "I honestly don't know. She's not exactly acting like a teenager in mourning."

"No. That's definitely true." Jared wiped at the corners of his mouth. "She seems callous. That's the best word I can think of to describe her."

"But if she's not getting an inheritance, what's her motive?" Shawn asked.

"She didn't know she wasn't getting the inheritance," Jared answered. "She seemed to think she had money coming her way and she was freaking ticked off when she realized that wasn't true."

"I think 'ticked off' is putting it mildly," Zander offered, licking his spoon. "She's been nothing but terrible the two times Harper and I saw her since Henry's death. Harp even gave her an out and said it was okay if she didn't want to put on an act in front of her friends, but the kid really is that rotten."

"The problem is that teenagers are a different breed," Jared volunteered. "There's a reason they can't be psychologically profiled. Half of them come across as sociopaths even if they're not really suffering from that mental defect."

"Is that true?" Harper furrowed her brow and offered Jared a bite of her ice cream since he was done with his share of the pumpkin-flavored goodness.

Jared happily took the bite and nodded. "Totally true. Psychological testing on anyone under the age of eighteen is considered iffy at best. Most judges won't take it into consideration. In fact, I once heard about a kid testing as a sociopath at the age of thirteen but testing normal at nineteen. He then went on to start a homeless shelter for abused teens and is regarded as something of a saint on the streets. He still tested as sociopathic at thirteen, though."

Harper widened her eyes. "Is that true?"

"Yes."

"Wow."

"Yeah, teenagers are entitled jerks a lot of the time, but their hormones are whacked out and sometimes you catch them on a bad day," Jared said. "So, while Marley might appear not to care ... we can't be certain that she doesn't care."

"So what do we do?" Zander asked.

"You don't do anything."

"Yeah, let's come back from La-La Land and be realistic," Zander drawled. "Harper isn't going to give this up. It happened too close to the house. I mean ... Henry's house is practically right on top of ours. It's kind of like Whisper Cove's version of *Three's Company* and he was Mr. Furley."

"I have no idea what that means," Jared admitted.

"Don Knotts on *Three's Company*," Harper supplied. "He was the landlord of the apartment building. Zander loves that show."

"I'll take your word for it," Jared said dryly. "As for the case, I would prefer if you would stay out of it."

Harper pursed her lips as she stared at the kitchen table, causing Jared to force out a sigh.

"Since I know you're not going to be able to stay out of this, I'm going to change my stance ... a little."

Harper flicked a pair of hopeful eyes in his direction. "Really?"

"I don't want you working on this because it might turn dangerous, but I know that you can't stop yourself from doing it," Jared clarified. "So, if you're going to work on it, I need you to promise to be careful."

Harper smiled as she threw her arms around his neck. "Thank you."

Jared made a face as he patted her back. "You're welcome."

Zander, on the other hand, merely offered up an imperious glance. "We don't need your permission."

"Perhaps it simply makes me feel better to give it," Jared said.

"Whatever." Zander rolled his eyes until they landed on Shawn. "Are you ready for bed? I'm officially exhausted."

Shawn nodded without hesitation. "I am. Once we're there, I figure we could talk about the fact that you lied to me, too."

Zander was blasé. "I didn't lie to you because I wanted to lie to you. I lied because I didn't have a choice. Harper was lying to Jared and you were unfortunate fodder. I knew you wouldn't care what we were doing."

"Oh, well, as long as you had a reason."

Jared shook his head as he watched them go, finally shifting his eyes to Harper. She looked cute and sweet as she stared at him. She also looked unbelievably weary. "You've had a long day."

"So have you."

"Do you want to wrap it up together and head to bed?"

Harper bobbed her head. "Yeah. Just one thing." She rested her hand on Jared's wrist to still him. "I'm sorry I lied. I'll do better. I promise."

Jared hated the earnest expression on her face. "Well, it wasn't a big lie."

"It was still a lie."

"And yet I love you anyway." He gave her a soft kiss. "We're going to figure all this out. I don't want you sitting around worrying."

Harper narrowed her eyes to suspicious slits. "What makes you think I'm sitting around worrying?"

Jared thought about his conversation with Zander and shrugged. "I just know you." He grabbed her hand. "Come on. I want to put this sugar buzz to good use before we both crash."

"Now that sounds like a plan."

HARPER FELL ASLEEP WITHOUT DIFFICULTY, BUT SHE WOKE three hours later for no apparent reason. She stared at the ceiling for a long beat, listening, and ultimately rolled to a sitting position and stared into the dark corner of the bedroom.

"I know you're here," she whispered.

Henry's ghost stepped forward, his expression amused. "I didn't mean to wake you. I didn't realize you would be asleep."

"It's the middle of the night. That's generally when I sleep."

"That's not how it felt for me when I watched your house. You guys used to stay up until all hours of the night when I was alive."

Harper pressed the heel of her hand to her forehead. "Didn't you go to bed at like nine o'clock?"

"Yes."

"So anything after that felt like the middle of the night to you, right?"

"It's better to get an early start on the day."

"Right. It doesn't matter." Harper rolled her neck until it cracked. "I really am tired, though. Do you have a specific reason for being here?"

"I do." Henry bobbed his head and floated toward the end of the bed. "I know you were at the cemetery tonight."

"How do you know that? Wait ... have you been following me? That's a little invasive. You might want to stop doing that if you want me to help."

"I wasn't following *you*."

Henry's jab was pointed. "Oh. You were following Marley. That makes more sense."

"I kind of wish I hadn't followed her," Henry admitted. "She's an extremely aimless young woman who has no purpose in life."

Despite her overt dislike for Marley, Harper found herself instinctively standing up for the girl. "She's young. You always find stupid things to waste time on when you're young. She'll outgrow that."

"I hope so." Henry looked whimsical. "You were following her because you thought she might've killed me, weren't you?"

"Do you still think it was assassins?"

"I *know* it was assassins."

"You were poisoned with arsenic and that can cause delusions. I think that's what we're dealing with here."

"No. It was really assassins. I know things." Henry tapped his ethereal head for emphasis. "It was the Russians. I'm sure of it now."

"Okay, well ... ." Harper licked her lips as she debated how to proceed. "I'm going to see what I can figure out tomorrow. We're at a standstill for now."

"I guess that's to be expected. You are blond, after all."

Harper scowled. "You are the rudest guy ever. You know that, right?"

"I prefer the term blunt."

Harper barely managed to contain her temper, and only because Jared slumbered next to her and she didn't want to wake him. "Just one question before you go."

"And what is that?"

"Why did Marley think she was getting a big inheritance?"

Henry shrugged, his demeanor shifting. "Because I told her she was."

"And why didn't you follow through with that?"

"Because I knew she would blow through anything I left her. I'm not an idiot. I wanted her to spend time with me so I offered up the bribe. That's why she was always around."

"That seems like a lame way to get attention."

"I wasn't looking for attention. I was looking for a way to make sure she didn't get in too much trouble. She's not a very bright kid, if you haven't noticed. I had to force her hand and make sure she spent time with me."

"She might've wanted to spend time with you if you didn't say things like 'she's not a very bright kid.'"

"I doubt it." Henry didn't look bothered by Harper's admonishment. "I lied to get her to hang out with me. I wanted to talk to her, feel her out, enlighten her about the realities of life."

"Oh, well, that sounds downright terrible. No wonder you had to bribe her to spend time with you."

Henry ignored the dig. "It worked out well for me."

"Yes, well, she's ticked now that she knows she's not getting anything. If you thought you were going to leave her with fond memories, you were wrong."

"I don't really care what memories I left her with. I just want her to turn out better than her mother."

Harper didn't bother to hide her scowl. "Carol is a good person. You verbally beat her down her entire life and yet she still loves you."

"She couldn't hold on to her husband."

"Her husband was a cheater. Why should she want to hold on to that guy?"

"If she'd done things right, he wouldn't have wanted to cheat."

"Oh, that's such crap." Harper rolled her eyes and sucked in a breath. "Your daughter makes excuses for you – like you have OCD and can't help yourself from being blunt – but at a certain point you realized you were being rude and simply didn't care."

"So?"

"So you're a douche." Harper settled back on her pillow. "I'm still going to help you, Henry, because that's what I do. You're not a nice man, though. In fact, you're kind of terrible. It's too late to adjust your attitude in life but you have a chance to do it in death."

"And why would I want to do that?"

"Because the best lesson you can learn as a person is that change isn't necessarily a bad thing."

"Is that why you date three different men? You like a little change in your life, don't you?"

Harper bit back a nasty retort. "I date one man."

"There are three under this roof."

"And the other two are in a different bed."

"That's all smoke and mirrors."

"Ugh." Harper slapped her hand to her forehead. "We really are living in *Three's Company*. That's how it feels sometimes."

"That was a terrible show," Henry sniffed.

"And you're a terrible man. Now ... go away. I'll talk to you more tomorrow but only during daylight hours."

"Fine. I'll see you then."

"I'm looking forward to it."

❧ 14 ❧

FOURTEEN

"What are you guys doing today?"
Jared finished his breakfast before asking the obvious question the next morning.

"We're decorating," Zander answered right away.

"We're hanging out with Henry's ghost and trying to figure out who he ticked off," Harper corrected, ignoring the dirty look Zander shot her. "I promised to be honest, so I'm being honest."

"Good girl." Jared smirked as he poked her side. "Where do you think you'll be doing that?"

"Probably here and across the road."

"How can you be sure he'll stop by?"

"Because he popped up in my bedroom again last night while you were sleeping and we made a plan."

Jared's smile shifted. "You were up talking to him again last night?"

"Does that bother you?"

"It bothers me that I didn't hear you," Jared admitted. "I'm a trained police officer. You would think I would take notice of these things."

Harper shrugged, unruffled. "I think you're simply getting used to life with me and you know the difference between when I'm in danger and merely working. I wouldn't worry about it."

"Well, I can't help being a little worried about it," Jared said. "Still, you're right. There's nothing to get worked up about."

"At least not yet," Zander clarified. "We haven't really gotten down and dirty with Henry yet. That's still to come."

Jared fought the urge to snap at Zander. "I'll work on waking up when you're talking in the middle of the night, Heart. I'm not sure what my problem is."

"I don't want you to wake up when you need sleep," Harper argued. "It wasn't a very interesting conversation anyway. He's kind of a douche."

Jared cocked an eyebrow. "How?"

"He's mean and he says whatever comes to his mind."

Jared flicked a pointed glance toward Zander. "I would think you'd be used to that."

"Hey!" Zander extended a warning finger. "I'm not mean."

"You're not exactly nice."

"I'm honest," Zander clarified. "I don't purposely try to be mean, though."

"He doesn't," Harper agreed. "He's honest but sweet. He's also loyal and he knows how to stroke an ego or two."

"Do you need your ego stroked?" Jared asked, genuinely curious.

Harper shrugged. "No. But it's still nice when it happens from time to time."

"I guess that's fair," Jared rubbed the back of his neck as he considered the day ahead of him. "Do you promise to be careful when you're running around with Henry's ghost?"

Harper nodded without hesitation. "Absolutely."

"Then have fun."

Now it was Harper's turn to be dubious. "That's it? You're not going to give me a hard time for this?"

"I'm going to be thankful you told me the truth and trust you're not going to do anything dangerous."

"Oh, wow, it's like absolute freedom," Zander drawled.

Jared refused to be baited into a fight. "You're free to do whatever you want whenever you want, Zander. If you run into danger, I'm fine with it."

"I'm not fine with it," Shawn countered.

Jared ignored him. "I don't want my Heart here running into danger because I would be crushed if something happened to her," he continued. "I want her safe. I'm funny like that. Sue me."

"Oh, you're so cute," Zander cooed, making a face. "I love how you worry about her but are fine with me dying."

"I didn't say dying," Jared clarified. "I wouldn't be okay with you dying. I'm simply not equipped to constantly worry about you because I'm not keen on getting an ulcer."

"Oh, I think that's the nicest thing you've ever said to me," Zander deadpanned.

"And I'm done." Jared let loose with an exasperated sigh as he turned to Harper. "Be good. Be careful. I love you."

Harper grinned. "Right back at you."

Jared leaned closer. "Oh, and you're the most beautiful woman in the world."

Harper widened her eyes to comical proportions. "Why did you add that part?"

"Because it's true."

"And?"

"And because maybe I wanted to stroke your ego, too."

Harper's grin widened. "I hit the jackpot when I found you."

"I think that goes for both of us." Jared gave her a quick kiss. "I have to get going. I'll be in touch if I stumble across any information you might find pertinent. You do the same for me, okay?"

"Absolutely." Harper grabbed his face and planted a wet kiss on his lips. "Have a good day."

"Ugh. I totally want to barf," Zander complained.

Shawn flicked his ear. "I think it's kind of sweet."

"Then you're delusional."

Shawn's response was mild. "I can live with that."

"SO ... THANKS FOR LAST NIGHT."

Jared was nervous as he entered the office area he shared with Mel and found his partner already toiling behind his desk.

"You're late." Mel's voice was unnaturally gruff.

Jared glanced at the clock. "According to that, I'm two minutes early."

"Well, you feel late."

Jared eased a doughnut bag onto the edge of Mel's desk and added a pumpkin latte to the mix. "I brought snacks."

Mel flicked his eyes to the offerings and made a face. "Do you think I can be bribed?"

"I'm hoping so."

The sigh Mel let loose was straight out of the "I'm sick of dealing with kids" playbook. "What kind of doughnut?"

"Cake with chocolate frosting."

"That's my favorite."

"I bought two of them for you."

Even though he was frustrated, Mel couldn't stop the smile from playing at the corners of his lips. "That's a pretty good bribe."

"This isn't my first time bribing a cop."

"I'm not sure you should be owning up to that."

"Yes, well ... ." Jared held his hands palms out and shrugged. "How angry are you?"

Mel was evasive. "What makes you think I'm angry?"

"Your face."

"My face is the same as it always is."

"Not really." Jared took the chair across from Mel's desk and fixed him with a rueful smile. "I'm sorry. I shouldn't have left you to deal with the kids last night, but I had my own set of kids to deal with and I honestly had no choice."

"Yeah. You turn into one of those kids when you spend too much time with Harper and Zander. It's not an attractive quality."

Jared balked. "Are you saying I'm immature?"

"Only when those two get you going."

"I'm not sure how you want me to fix that," Jared said after a beat. "I don't try to be immature when I'm with them. Sometimes it simply happens."

Mel wanted to remain stern, but one look at his partner's hangdog expression had him changing course. "It's not as if I blame you for everything that happened. I only blame you for half of it."

"Who do you blame for the other half?"

"Zander."

"What about Harper?"

Mel shrugged. "She's always been a good girl and she stands up for Zander whenever possible. She also keeps him busy so the rest of us don't have to deal with him so she's considered something of a saint when it comes to our family."

Jared smirked. "She does kind of look like an angel, doesn't she?"

"Ugh. You're so sickly sweet with her I can't stand it." Mel dug into the bag and came out with a doughnut. "What did you find out from them after I left?"

"Do you really want to know or are you just being polite?"

"I really want to know."

"Okay, well, it wasn't much." Jared turned serious. "Henry's ghost stopped in for a chat with Harper while I was sleeping last night and he essentially said he lied to Marley because he wanted her to hang out with him."

"That's a little sad," Mel noted. "Kids should always want to hang out with their grandparents."

"I don't get the feeling that Henry was particularly nice to Marley."

"What makes you say that?"

"Some of the things Harper has said," Jared replied. "She made it sound as if Henry was especially hard on the kid for doing teenager stuff ... like crushing on boys and fussing with hair and makeup. He also didn't seem to think she was very bright and then started talking bad about his daughter."

Mel exhaled heavily, making a clucking sound with his tongue as he shook his head. "Yeah. The thing with Henry is that he was never a pleasant guy. He didn't just say those things to family members. He said them to anyone who would listen."

"So we have a guy who made enemies from one end of the town to the other through his job but died after he retired," Jared mused. "I'm not sure what to make of it."

"I'm not sure what to make of it either," Mel admitted. "The good news is, the full report from the medical examiner's office should be here within the hour. Hopefully that will give us more to go on."

"Hopefully." Jared smiled as he leaned forward. "We're good, right?"

Mel nodded. "We're good."

"Great. Give me that other doughnut."

Mel grabbed the bag and clutched it to his chest. "You'll have to kill me for this doughnut. I'm not joking. This is mine and you can't have it."

"You're just as much of a pain as your nephew."

"You take that back!"

"STOP BEING A PAIN, ZANDER." HARPER PLANTED HER hands on her hips as she stood in front of Henry's house and watched her best friend carry on from thirty feet away. "There's nothing in those bushes that's going to hop out and grab you."

Zander rolled his eyes. "I didn't say it was going to hop out. I said something was going to hop on ... like bugs. There are bugs in bushes, Harp. You know how I feel about bugs."

"Yeah, yeah, yeah." Harper wrinkled her nose. "They're a blight on humanity and should be eradicated. You've told me a hundred times."

"And yet you act as if it's news to you each and every time we discuss it," Zander complained. "Bugs are evil. I don't want any animal to go extinct ... except for bugs. They're gross and serve no purpose."

"They serve a lot of purpose, like pollination," Harper countered. "They also serve as a source of nourishment for things like bats, frogs and even bears. You love bears."

Zander planted his hands on his hips. "I like teddy bears. Let's not start exaggerating, okay?"

Harper snorted. "Fine. You like teddy bears. That doesn't mean insects aren't important."

"I don't care what you say," Zander shot back. "Bugs are evil and there are bugs in this bush."

Harper tamped down her out-of-control irritation. "Do you see bugs?"

"I don't have to see them to know they're there. Bugs hide under branches and can make themselves invisible. Then, even after a long search and when you think it's safe, they attack and try to kill you."

"They make themselves invisible?"

"What? That's a thing." Zander was unnaturally screechy. "I saw it on a documentary. Bugs make themselves invisible and lull you into a false sense of security and then ... bam! ... they appear out of nowhere and give you diseases and stuff."

"What kind of diseases are you talking about?"

"Um ... malaria, for one."

"I haven't heard of an outbreak of malaria in this area all summer," Harper deadpanned. "Now. Come on. You need to get into that bush and see if you can see me walking into Henry's house from that angle. Jack claimed he saw shadows the night before Henry was found, which means someone was sneaking around and we somehow missed it."

"I don't know how that could possibly happen given how interested you guys are in everything that occurs in this neighborhood," Shawn noted. He sat in a chair ten feet behind Zander and grinned as he watched the show.

"Don't you have work to do?" Zander snapped.

Shawn shook his head. "I'm yours all day."

"Well, that's lovely." Zander rolled his eyes. "As for the malaria, just because you haven't heard about it, that doesn't mean it's not happening. The government hides malaria cases."

"Did you hear that on television, too?" Harper asked dryly.

"As a matter of fact I did." Zander wrinkled his nose as he moved closer to the bush, squinting as he turned his attention back to Harper. "I can totally see you."

"I figured." Harper made a face. "I don't understand how we missed it if someone really did go inside Henry's house that night."

"We weren't looking out the window that night," Shawn pointed out. "We were watching a movie."

"Still ... you would think we would hear something," Harper said, rubbing her chin. "We need to talk to Henry about the people who hated him. Where is he?"

"You rang?" Henry asked dryly, popping into view at Harper's elbow and causing her to jolt.

"Don't do that!" Harper snapped, slapping at air. "You scared the crap out of me."

Shawn was instantly alert as he hopped to his feet. "What's going on?"

"She's talking to Henry," Zander replied, focusing on the bush. "Come over here and help me search for invisible bugs. She'll tell us what's going on over there when she's done talking to him."

Shawn didn't look convinced. "Do you want me to go over there, Harper?"

Harper didn't immediately answer, instead keeping her focus on something only she could see. "Where have you been?"

"I don't know." Henry was annoyed. "I can't always control my comings and goings. I'm new to this."

Harper had the grace to be abashed. "I'm sorry about that. It's not your fault and I feel bad for jumping all over you."

"Whatever." Henry flicked his eyes to Zander. "What are your boyfriends doing?"

"Trying to help. We can't figure out how someone got into your house without us noticing. We should've at least heard someone park in the driveway or on the street. This is a tiny dead-end street and there are only three houses on it, for crying out loud. Do you remember anyone parking that night?"

"I already told you it was assassins." Henry's tone was dry. "Assassins know what they're doing so they don't make noise."

"Yeah. It's not assassins." Harper tapped her sneaker-clad toe on the ground. "Who have you ticked off recently?"

"That's a really long list."

Harper was afraid he would say that. "Well, we still need to hear it. We're treading water and there is no lifeboat in sight. We need a direction to focus."

"Okay, but I've made a lot of enemies."

"Trust me. We know."

"You asked for it."

"IS THAT THE MEDICAL EXAMINER'S REPORT?"

Jared lifted his head and watched as Mel flipped through a freshly-delivered report.

Mel nodded.

"Anything of interest?" Jared prodded.

"I guess it depends on what you find interesting," Mel replied.

"Try me."

"Okay. For starters, Henry wasn't killed by arsenic."

Jared made an exaggerated face. "But they said he was poisoned."

"He was still poisoned, it simply wasn't arsenic," Mel explained. "The arsenic test alerted, but I guess that's common with certain types of poisons. In this case, it alerted because the poison used was organic."

"I don't know what that means." Jared rested his weight on his elbows and leaned forward. "If it's not arsenic, what was it?"

"Some fertilizer that's been out of commission for ten years." Mel remained focused on the report. "It's toxic and was banned more than a decade ago. No one carries it ... and I don't mean just locally. It's been banned countrywide."

"Huh." Jared had no idea what to make of the twist. "So we're looking for a killer who had access to fertilizer from a decade ago."

"Pretty much."

"That narrows things down but almost too much. How are we supposed to track down fertilizer that shouldn't legally exist?"

"I don't know. I need to think on it." Mel pressed his tongue against the back of his teeth. "It's weird, right?"

"What?"

"Henry worked for code enforcement, which generally deals with lawn maintenance and house repairs, and then he was killed by fertilizer ... which someone would use for lawn maintenance."

Jared shrugged. "It could be a coincidence. If that fertilizer was pulled for being toxic, it was probably big news back in the day. Maybe whoever kept it had a reason for keeping the stuff."

"Like he or she was planning on going after Henry for a long time and only finally put the plan into action?"

Mel shrugged. "It's a theory."

"It is. Until we can figure out where someone would get that stuff, though, that's all we've got."

"So ... let's track it down." Mel was resigned as he turned back to his computer. "Let's put together a list of places that would keep unusable fertilizer for a decade."

"That's bound to be a short list."

"That's all we got."

15

FIFTEEN

"**O**h, good. It's my two favorite people."

Jason Thurman met Harper and Zander by the front door of his beach restaurant, beaming from ear to ear. His expression immediately made Zander suspicious.

"Whatever it is, I didn't do it."

Jason snorted as he clapped Zander on the shoulder. "What makes you think I believe you did anything?"

Zander shrugged. "I've met you. You're a world-class thunder stealer, which means you probably suspect people of doing things they didn't really do every single day of your life. I bet that's right up your alley."

Harper shot Zander a quelling look. "Don't start with the thunder stealer stuff again. I thought you were over that."

"I thought so, too." Jason's expression was rueful. "Don't worry about Zander offending me, though. I'm used to his shtick."

"Hey, I'm a chameleon. My shtick never stays the same."

Harper studied her best friend for a long beat. "That came out dirtier than you expected, didn't it?"

"Totally."

"That's what I thought." Harper rolled her neck as she followed

Jason toward a small table in the corner. "Actually, we're going to need a bigger table. We're four today."

Jason arched an eyebrow. "And yet I only see two of you."

"Shawn and Jared are coming," Harper explained.

"Jared, huh?" Jason didn't bother to hide his disappointment. In high school, he dated Harper for a cool couple of weeks before breaking her heart and moving. When he returned to Whisper Cove, he was hopeful he might get another shot. That notion flew out of his head the moment he saw Harper and Jared together.

"I thought you liked Jared now." Harper shrugged out of her coat and draped it over the back of her chair. "Last time I checked, you guys were at least pretending to be buddies."

"I like him fine," Jason lied. "I think he's a pip of a guy."

"Are you sure you're not gay?" Zander asked, taking everyone by surprise with the conversational shift.

"Quite sure."

"Only gay guys use the word 'pip.' I think you're gay and the real reason you constantly stole my thunder when we were younger is because you were in love with me and that was the only way you could get my attention."

Jason blinked several times in rapid succession. "I see."

"That's also the reason you dated Harper, in case you're interested," Zander added. "You wanted to steal my best friend so I would feel love's keen burn the same way you did."

Jason merely rolled his eyes. "Has anyone ever told you that your imagination is something to be revered?"

"I tell myself that every day." Zander took a seat next to Harper and let his gaze bounce around the restaurant. "I see you went all out for Halloween. The decorations are truly breathtaking."

Since he hadn't changed a thing, Jason knew exactly what Zander was getting at. "It's being done Sunday morning, smart guy," he shot back. "I hired a company to come in and do it for me."

"Wait ... people actually pay other people to decorate for them?" Zander was intrigued. "Harp, I think we missed our calling. We should be doing that instead of chasing ghosts."

Harper focused on her menu. "At least we have a fallback plan should we ever need one. What kind of soup do you have today, Jason?"

"A beautiful butternut squash and clam chowder."

"Yum. I like squash soup."

"It's really good. In fact ... ."

Zander, already bored with the conversation, decided to take it over. "What are you dressing up as this Halloween?"

Jason considered pointing out how rude Zander was but understood it was a wasted effort. "I haven't decided yet. I'm thinking about going as James Bond, though."

"Fancy." Harper grinned. "Do you have a tuxedo?"

"I do. I think I'll look smashing dressed up as everyone's favorite spy."

"Just don't run around and pretend you're an assassin," Zander said. "Although, you might want to be careful. If you put on a tuxedo everyone is far more likely to think you're a waiter than a spy."

Jason ignored the dig. "Why would I want to pretend I'm an assassin?"

"Because the ghost we're helping right now thinks he was killed by assassins," Zander replied. Jason was in on the big secret so he wasn't worried about discussing Harper's abilities with their former classmate.

"Assassins, huh?" Jason was genuinely amused as he flicked his gaze to the door and waved at Jared and Shawn. "I think your guests have arrived."

Harper glanced over her shoulder and smiled. "They're kind of handsome, huh?"

"I would only date a handsome man," Zander supplied. "I could never date someone ugly. I'm shallow like that."

"You really don't have to tell people you're shallow," Jason noted. "I think they can figure that out for themselves while talking to you."

Zander made a face and stuck out his tongue. His relationship with Jason was better than when the man first returned to town, but it was hardly the stuff of bromance dreams. "You're on my last nerve."

"I believe that's my permanent home," Jason teased. "Welcome, gentlemen. It's so nice that you decided to grace my humble establishment."

Shawn sent Jason a curious look as he sat on the other side of Zander. "What are you talking about?"

"He's clearly hard up for attention," Zander replied. "This is the way he gets it. He doesn't care if it's negative or positive ... just that he gets it."

"He sounds like someone else I know," Jared said pointedly, dropping a quick kiss on Harper's upturned mouth as he sat. "You look the same as when I left – other than a little extra color in your cheeks – so I'm guessing you didn't get into any trouble while I was gone."

"Define trouble," Zander prodded.

Harper scalded him with a dark look before focusing her full attention on Jared. "We basically spent the entire morning trying to approach Henry's house from different angles because we don't understand how we missed either one or more killers entering his house."

"Are you talking about Henry Spencer?" Jason asked.

Harper nodded. "He was poisoned and we're trying to help his ghost find closure."

"You know, Harp, I don't think you should be spreading our private business around town to every Tom, Dick, or Jason who asks a question," Zander said. "He might share some of our secrets if we're not careful."

Jason narrowed his eyes. "Why would I share your secrets?"

"And what secrets?" Jared challenged. "You guys put every single thing you do on those brochures you have at the grocery store and library. What secrets is Jason possibly going to tell?"

"I just want to point out that you're the one who mentioned ghosts first, too, Zander," Harper added. "You can't have it both ways."

Zander narrowed his eyes and folded his arms in front of him. "I don't think I like everyone's attitudes."

"You'll survive." Shawn patted his boyfriend's arm in a superficial manner before locking gazes with Jared. "I helped them all morning and I'm not sure what they managed to accomplish with their day so far. All I can say is that they're right on part of it. No one parked at Henry's house without us noticing.

"I don't care if we were in the middle of a movie or already in bed," he continued. "You can't miss the sound of a car on that shared driveway. It's gravel. We tested it back and forth several times."

Jared chuckled. "It sounds as if you guys had a full day."

"We were merely being scientific," Harper hedged. "You might think it's a waste of time, but we wanted to work things out for ourselves."

Jared was instantly contrite. "I'm sorry, Heart. I simply thought the idea of you guys testing sounds and racing up and down the driveway sounded cute. I admire your scientific approach."

Harper didn't believe him for a second. "Whatever. We found it helpful."

"We did," Zander agreed, bobbing his head. "No matter what, headlights would've hit Harper's bedroom window. We know you wouldn't wake – not even if someone were say ... talking in the same room while you slept – but Harper is a light sleeper. She would've seen the light. That's the side of the bed she sleeps on, too."

"How do you know which side of the bed she sleeps on?" Jason was legitimately curious. "I thought your room was across the hall."

"It is but we all spend an inordinate amount of time together in bed on weekday mornings," Jared said dryly. "Everyone has a specific spot."

"Oh, don't do that whining thing you do," Zander groused. "I promised I would stay out of her bed when you're there. What more do you want from me?"

The admission caught Jared off guard. "You did?"

"Have I been in bed with you the past few days?"

Jared swallowed hard. "Actually ... no."

"So what is it you're complaining about?"

"I don't know." Jared felt mildly stupid. "I'm sorry for saying that in the first place given the fact that you've been so good lately. I retract every bad thing I've ever said about you."

"Even the time you said I was dramatic?"

"No. I said every *bad* thing I said about you. That's true and it's not really bad."

Zander's eyes flashed. "I am not dramatic!"

Jared and Jason broke into twin guffaws while Shawn let loose with a challenging mouth swish.

"Zander, you spent twenty minutes talking about invisible bugs this afternoon," Shawn pointed out. "If that's not dramatic, what is?"

"Oh, I can't even deal with you people," Zander muttered, finding a spot on the wall to stare at while he worked to tamp down his irritation. "You all make me sick to my stomach."

"Poor Zander." Jason patted his shoulder. "I don't think it sounds like you're having a good day. Do you want some squash soup to make you feel better?"

"It's going to take more than that."

"If you want to start day drinking, I'm okay with that, too," Jason said. "Just tell me what you want."

"You're not day drinking," Harper warned. "We have other stuff to do this afternoon, including looking through the woods behind Henry's house for tracks, so you can't drink."

"Whatever." Zander's irritation was on full display. "I'm done talking to all of you for the duration of lunch."

"That sounds horrible," Jared deadpanned before focusing on Harper. "Why are you going through the woods?"

"Because someone approached that house to kill Henry."

"You don't know that the poison wasn't slipped into Henry's pocket or something," Jared argued. "We have no idea when Henry ingested it ... or how. Speaking of which ... ."

Harper ignored the fact that Jared was about to continue. "Jack saw someone going into Henry's house the night before we found him dead. It was after dark and Jack said that whoever it was acted furtive. That was his word, not mine."

"Let's hope so," Jared muttered. "As for Jack, how much do you think a hundred-year-old ghost really knows? I mean ... why was he paying attention in the first place?"

"He hangs around our house all the time."

"That is creepy."

"I like that you think it's creepy that the ghost hangs out at their

141

house, but you're not bothered by the fact that she talks to ghosts all the time while at work," Jason noted. "What's that about?"

"Yeah, what is that about?" Zander asked.

Jared shrugged. "She's complicated and special. That's why I love her. The pirate ghost thing is hard for me to understand, though. Why is he still hanging around?"

"He doesn't want to cross over," Harper replied. "There's no reason to force him when he's behaving himself. When he's ready, I'll help him. Until then ... what do you want me to do?"

"Nothing more than you're doing." Jared captured her hand and pressed her fingers to his lips. "If you want to wander around the woods looking for prints, knock yourself out. On the poison front, though, I do have a bit of an update."

Harper stilled. "Really?" She sensed Jared was unhappy sharing whatever news he had and yet he was resigned to doing it all the same. "What's your update?"

"It seems Henry wasn't killed by arsenic after all."

Harper's mouth dropped open. "Are you about to tell me he died of natural causes? If so, I know you're lying and we just had a talk last night about honesty."

"We did, and you were the one lying," Jared reminded her. "As for natural causes, that's a big no. Henry was still poisoned, it simply wasn't arsenic."

"What was it?" Shawn asked, furrowing his brow.

"Some fertilizer that was outlawed ten years ago because it was making people sick and even killing a few of them," Jared answered. "It's been off the market for a decade, and yet somehow it ended up inside of Henry."

"Holy crap," Harper muttered. "But ... how?"

"Your guess is as good as mine. We're trying to track down places that might have the stuff stashed away somewhere, but it's not exactly easy."

"It doesn't sound all that hard," Zander challenged.

"Oh, really?" Jared pinned him with a dark gaze. "Name one place that would have that fertilizer just sitting around."

"How about the abandoned school utility building?" Zander shot back.

Jared flicked his eyes to Harper. "What's that?"

"It's actually a good answer," Harper replied. "I know you don't want to hear it but ... Zander might be on to something."

"He really might," Jason agreed.

"Now I'm starting to like you again." Zander beamed at Jason. "It's because you're ready to admit you're gay and in love with me, right?"

Shawn made an incredulous face. "What?"

"Just ignore him," Harper ordered, waving her hand.

"Yes, ignore him and focus on me," Jared instructed. "What is this building you're talking about?"

"It's kind of like the old bus barn," Harper explained. "Do you know where the football field is?"

Jared nodded. "It has a building on the other side of it. Is that the building you're talking about?"

"No. Fifteen years ago, the football field was on the other side of the school. You probably don't realize it because the old field is covered with trees now, but those trees are fairly young and were purposely planted."

"Okay." Jared wasn't sure what they were getting at. "Why?"

"It was a whole big thing about the field retaining water during storms or something," Harper replied. "That part doesn't matter. What does matter is that there's a rundown building in those trees that no one pays attention to."

"Okay ... and you're saying that building will have the fertilizer in it?"

"It might," Harper replied. "That's where they kept everything for the football field."

"And what's in it now?" Jared asked, rubbing his chin. "Have you been inside?"

"I have no reason to go inside. It's not haunted as far as I know. However, I don't believe they moved all the landscaping supplies from it. So, if there was a good place to start looking for old supplies ... ."

"That would be it," Jared finished, flicking a set of impressed eyes to Zander. "You actually came up with a good tip."

Zander haughtily studied his fingernails. "You seem surprised."

"I'm just ... thankful."

"Well, then you're about to be doubly thankful," Jason interjected, drawing four sets of curious eyes to him. "I think I might know where more of that fertilizer is."

"Where is that?" Jared asked.

"Yeah, where is that?" Zander snapped.

"Under my deck," Jason replied. "I happened to be there yesterday because I'm having a big Halloween party at the end of the month and I wanted to talk to the decoration company about putting lights down there."

"And you found something?" Jared prodded.

Jason nodded. "I didn't think much of it at the time because I figured it was kids hanging out underneath there. There was fertilizer, though. It looked old."

"Well, that's definitely interesting." Jared rolled his neck. "What makes you think kids were hanging out underneath there?"

"Because there were also packages of toilet paper, shaving cream, and eggs," Jason replied. "It's vandalism month in Whisper Cove. I'm old, but I still remember what it was like to be a kid. Those are mainstays around Halloween."

"Huh." Jared let his eyes drift to Harper. "That changes things a bit, doesn't it?"

"I guess it depends on what kids are hanging around under the deck," Harper replied. "If Marley was one of them ... yeah, it changes things."

"I'm going to need to take a look under your deck, Jason." Jared slowly got to his feet. "I might have to call for backup, too."

"Better now instead of close to the party," Jason said, resigned. "I'll take you down."

"You do that, thunder stealer," Zander hissed, narrowing his eyes.

"Why are we back to that?" Jason was understandably confused.

"I was the hero of lunch hour until you swooped in and stole my glory."

"Oh." Jason shrugged. "If I give you free squash soup, are we square?"

Zander shook his head. "I want fresh bread, too. I can't be bought off with soup alone."

"Done."

Zander's lips curved. "Then we're friends again."

Jason made a face. "You are truly a magnificent human being."

"I know."

16

SIXTEEN

"**S**o, what's the verdict?"

Harper was on pins and needles waiting for Jared to return home after his shift. She tried calling – twice – but both times he blew her off because he said he didn't have the information she was looking for. After that he stopped accepting her calls and she bordered on furious by the time he walked through the door.

Jared stared at her for a moment. "Is that any way to welcome the man you supposedly love?"

Harper internally debated yelling at him but knew that would get her nowhere fast. "Okay. Fine." She got to her feet and strode to him, helping him shrug out of his coat and hanging it in the closet before shoving him to the couch and yanking off his shoes.

Jared arched an eyebrow, amusement and annoyance warring. Delight in the look on Harper's face won out. "Thank you, darling. I appreciate the warm welcome."

"Yeah, yeah, yeah." Harper threw the shoes toward the door, ignoring the fact that they landed on the carpet rather than the rug. "Can I get you anything else?"

"A beer would be nice."

Harper narrowed her eyes to dangerous blue slits. "Are you messing with me?"

"I've got the beer." Shawn disappeared into the kitchen, returning a few minutes later with a Corona and a smile. "Would you like a foot rub with that?" he asked Jared as he delivered it.

Jared tilted his head to the side, considering. "Not from you. I hope that doesn't hurt your feelings."

"Something tells me I'll live," Shawn said dryly.

"I guess I will, too." Jared flashed a smirk for Harper's benefit. "So, Heart, tell me about your day. What did you do after lunch?"

Harper was so agitated she considered throwing herself on Jared and poking him in the chest until he started delivering answers. Since she knew that's what he wanted – it would essentially turn into a win for him – she sucked in a calming breath.

"Well, I spent the afternoon in the woods looking for tracks with Zander and Shawn." Harper's voice was unnaturally cold.

"Did you find anything?"

"Zander thought he found a dead body."

Jared jolted. "What? Why didn't you call me?"

"Because it turned out to be an old bread bag," Harper replied. "He always thinks he discovers a body whenever we go into the woods. I have no idea why."

"It looked like a body," Zander protested, appearing in the doorway that separated the living and dining rooms, a spatula in his hand. "Laugh all you want, Harp, but you thought it was a body, too."

Jared didn't bother hiding his amusement as he pinned Harper with a questioning look. "Did you think it was a body?"

"No. I was considering killing Zander and actually leaving his body there, but I didn't believe it was a body."

"I knew it wasn't a body, too," Shawn offered. "I also knew Harper was seriously considering killing Zander – what with the raccoon incident and all – so I threw my body between them and averted a murder. I'm a hero."

Jared chuckled. "The more time you spend with Zander, the more you act like him. Has anyone ever told you that?"

"I believe you told me that exact thing twice this week."

"I did," Jared amiably agreed.

"Hey, that's a good thing," Zander argued. "The whole world wants to be like me. If they had a magazine called Everyday Heroes, I would be on the cover every month. That's how awesome I am."

Shawn sent him a flirty wink. "I would buy each issue, too."

"Oh, geez." Jared rubbed his forehead, irritation creeping in. "Are Harper and I that annoying when we flirt?"

"Ten times more," Zander answered.

"Lesson learned." Jared reached over and tugged on the ends of Harper's blond hair. "Is that all you did?"

"Are you trying to kill me?" Harper exploded, her inner diva taking over. She grabbed Jared's hand and gave his wrist a vicious squeeze. "You're trying to drive me insane, aren't you? That's the only explanation for why you're acting like this."

It took a lot of effort, but Jared remained calm. "Whatever do you mean, Heart?"

"Do you want me to wrestle you down and smother you?"

"I like the wrestling idea."

"Jared." Harper adopted a whiny tone that would've grated a lesser man. Jared couldn't hold out against her misery, though, and instead leaned forward to give her a quick kiss.

"I guess it's time I gave you an update, huh?"

"Definitely." Harper enthusiastically bobbed her head. "Was the fertilizer a match?"

"It was."

"Ha!" Harper raised her fist in triumph, allowing a sheepish smile to tug at the corners of her mouth when she realized how obnoxious she was acting. "I sometimes spend too much time with Zander and absorb his mannerisms, too."

"I've learned to live with it." Jared leaned back on the couch. "The fertilizer is definitely what we're looking for."

"Oh, well, that's just great," Zander groused, wrinkling his forehead. "The thunder stealer struck again."

"Is it so bad that Jason was right?" Jared asked.

"We'll see how much you like Jason being right when he moves on your girlfriend a second time."

"Yeah, we've talked about that and he's not going to do it again. He knows I'll kill him if he tries."

"Oh, he's not afraid of you," Zander shot back. "He sees you as a big marshmallow because you're such a ball of fluff whenever you're around Harper."

"Well, if the s'more fits." Jared grinned before sighing. "There's something else. We decided to check the building by the school, the one you told me about, and the fertilizer was found inside there, too."

Harper's mouth dropped open. "So they were both right."

"Ha!" Zander pumped his fist while swinging his hips. "I was right, too. Where is Jason Thurman now?"

"I don't know." Jared remained calm. "If you think it will help, I'll go to the restaurant tomorrow and tell him you were both right. Is that what you want?"

Zander nodded without hesitation. "You can take a voice recorder and tape the conversation for me to listen to later. Make sure you comment so I know exactly when he cries."

"I'll consider it." Jared rubbed at the back of his neck. "It looks like whoever moved the fertilizer to the spot under Jason's deck took it from the building by the school."

"What makes you say that?" Shawn asked, sobering.

"The building was disturbed, footprints on the floor, and the door looked to have been jimmied. We talked to the superintendent and he claims no one goes in that building any longer. He says the janitors and landscapers keep all their equipment in the new building."

"Do you believe him?" Harper asked.

Jared nodded. "There was very little in that building. Mel brought up the fact that it should probably be torn down because it was nothing but a safety hazard – and a temptation for kids skipping school because they want to smoke on school grounds – but the principal says they don't have the money to tear it down. Mel said he would handle talking to city council, so if I have to guess, that building won't survive through Christmas."

"That doesn't do you a lot of good now," Harper noted. "Still, what's your next step."

"Tomorrow we interview Mike Dunlap. We tried to do it today, but his parents insisted he have an attorney present – and we do it in their home – so that's the first thing on our agenda tomorrow."

"Why Mike?"

"Because we already interviewed Marley."

That little tidbit caused Harper to jerk her head in excitement. "You did? What did she say? Wait ... did she suddenly cry crocodile tears and say she would never hurt her grandfather because she loved him? That would be just like the little monster."

"She didn't fake anything as far as I can tell," Jared countered. "She was just as defiant as she was at the cemetery last night."

"Huh." Harper rubbed her cheek as she shifted her legs and got comfortable next to Jared on the couch. "What did she say when you questioned her?"

"She denied hanging out beneath Jason's deck."

"That doesn't surprise you, does it?" Shawn asked. "She doesn't strike me as the stupid sort."

"She's not, but her mother called her out for lying to us," Jared said. "Carol stated that she's seen Marley in that exact spot at least twice in the last two weeks."

"She turned on her own daughter?" Zander mused. "That's cold."

"She didn't turn on her," Jared clarified. "She doesn't believe her daughter is guilty of anything but falling in with the wrong crowd. She made that very clear."

"That sounds about right," Harper supplied. "My mother pulled the same routine when I was a kid. I got caught smoking behind the gym and she blamed Zander."

"Yes, that was a lovely day," Zander agreed. "I tried telling her I wouldn't smoke because I didn't want my clothes to smell, but she didn't believe me. We were separated for a full week as punishment and it was the longest seven days of my entire life."

Jared pursed his lips to keep from laughing at Zander's hangdog expression. "Somehow you survived, though."

"Just barely."

"Did Marley own up to hanging out on the beach after her mother outed her?" Shawn asked.

"Yes and no," Jared hedged. "She says she was on the beach with

Mike – taking romantic walks on the sand and gazing into one another's eyes – but claims she was nowhere near the deck.

"She did point the finger at a couple of kids who were at the cemetery last night," he continued. "We talked to them, though, and they claim they were never at the beach and wouldn't go there because Mike insisted that was his private spot for romance. Apparently he's such a big deal that no one in Whisper Cove would dare go against him."

"That might be true," Harper hedged. "Whisper Cove is small. The quarterback of the football team has a lot of power in a very small circle. If Mike claimed that spot, the others might've actually stayed away."

"I'm not sure I believe them – and I definitely don't believe Marley – but we're kind of stuck until we talk to Mike tomorrow," Jared said. "I don't foresee him admitting to being a murderer, but I think there's a possibility we might get somewhere all the same."

Harper figured out what he was getting at before he could continue. "You think he's going to blame everything on Marley, don't you?"

"I think that's as good of a possibility as anything else. I mean, look at what we know. We know that Marley doesn't seem to care about her grandfather's death. We know that she promised her boyfriend a big gift to keep him loyal to her. We also know she had access to chemicals that shouldn't exist. It's not much of a stretch to believe that Mike is going to blame everything on her."

"So, basically, she did everything to hold onto a guy and he's going to roll over on her the first chance he gets," Harper mused. "That seems somehow ... depressing."

"Don't be depressed." Jared kissed the tip of her nose before swigging his beer. "I would go to jail if you killed someone and I knew about it. That's how loyal I am."

Harper rolled her eyes. "You're so full of crap. You're a cop. You wouldn't cover up a murder for me."

"That's not true." Jared was serious. "You're not the murdering sort. If you killed someone, you would have a good reason. I have faith in that ... and you. I would totally cover up for you."

Harper couldn't stop herself from being a little charmed. "And here I thought you were going to be annoying all night. Boy, was I wrong."

"I'm glad to hear it." Jared wiggled his feet as he rested them on the coffee table. "So ... about that foot massage."

Harper snorted. "Dream on."

"Ah, the love comes and goes in this house."

Harper kissed his cheek. "I'll play a different game with you later if that's what you want. I'm not rubbing your feet, though. That's too ... domestic."

"And we can't have that."

"Hey, I'll wear an apron when we play later," Harper offered.

"You will?"

"Yup. An apron and nothing else."

"And that right there is why I love you."

JARED LIGHTLY SNORED NEXT TO HER WHEN HARPER dragged herself from sleep shortly after midnight. She didn't have to search this time to know what woke her.

"What do you want, Henry?"

"I'm sorry to wake you." Henry looked sheepish.

"You don't look sorry." Harper ran a restless hand through her hair and clutched the covers close to her chest to make sure Henry didn't get a gander at anything he shouldn't see. "How long have you been here?"

"I dropped in earlier, but you were ... um ... busy. I left right away and only risked coming back now. Don't worry, I didn't see anything good."

"Uh-huh." Harper wasn't convinced as she leaned over the side of the bed and rooted around until she found a shirt. She tugged it over her head before releasing the blanket and leaning forward. "Do you have something you want to talk about?"

"It was still assassins."

"It wasn't assassins."

"It was."

"Henry ... ."

Henry made a throat-clearing sound, which was odd since he didn't technically have a throat, and waved off whatever Harper was going to say next. "It doesn't matter. I heard what you were talking about earlier, though. I just want to say ... you're wrong."

Harper licked her lips, debating. "You don't believe Marley killed you, do you?"

"No. She's my granddaughter. She's not capable of that."

"I have to tell you, I've spent a little time with her over the past few days. She's not a nice girl. In fact, she's something of a monster. Now, I can't decide if she's really that way or acts that way because you were mean to her, but she's extremely unpleasant."

"I wasn't mean to her," Henry protested.

"I don't believe you."

"Well, maybe I don't care what you believe. You have three boyfriends. It's not as if you're a sterling representative of the human race."

Harper made a disgusted face. "I don't have to put up with this. If you want to keep being a jerk, you can do it someplace else. I'm done with you."

"Oh, you can't be done." Henry shifted his attitude. "I don't mean to be rude. Sometimes I can't help it."

"Oh, I think you can help it. That's the big problem. You know you're being rude and you either don't care or enjoy it. I'm not sure which is worse."

"I swear I'll be better."

Harper considered arguing, but she was too weary. "Fine. We should have more information tomorrow. Stop by then ... during the day, when it's sunny out."

"It won't be Marley."

"I hope you're right. If it's her ... well, if it's her, it will be a terrible waste. I don't want it to be her any more than you do."

"I doubt that's true. That's not why I'm here, though."

"Oh?" Harper arched an eyebrow. "Why are you here? By the way, if you say something rude about me having three boyfriends again − which is completely untrue − I'm totally going to wash my hands of you. I'm not kidding."

"I'm here because there's someone in my house."

Harper blinked several times in rapid succession. "Excuse me."

Henry nodded, somber. "There's someone in my house."

"Right now?"

"Yes."

Harper wasn't sure she believed him, but curiosity got the better of her and she tossed the covers off her legs and crossed to the window, narrowing her eyes as she peered out into the darkness. She spent a full minute staring at Henry's dark home before speaking.

"I don't think anyone is over there."

"No. I saw a shadow. The assassins are back." Henry hovered close to Harper's side. "See. There. Right by the front door."

Harper squinted. "I ... ." She was about to call Henry crazy and return to bed when she caught sight of a hint of movement. "Son of a ... ." She swiveled quickly and crawled on the bed, grabbing Jared's arm to wake him.

"Again, Heart?" Jared's voice was thick with sleep. "You're an animal."

"Not that." Harper rolled her eyes. "Henry is here."

"Tell him to shut up and come back tomorrow."

"He can't do that." Harper kept her voice calm even though she wanted to scream at Jared to get up. "He says someone is at his house and I just looked myself and there's someone screwing around on the front porch."

"Okay, well ... ." Jared broke off and rolled to a sitting position, Harper's words cutting through the thick fog in his brain. "Are you sure?"

"Yes."

"Well, I guess having a ghost in the bedroom has finally paid off, huh? Let's see what we've got."

17

SEVENTEEN

J ared didn't find anyone on the front porch.

By the time he got to Henry's house, the property was deserted and all that was left behind was a pair of muddy footprints. Jared spent thirty minutes searching for signs of an intruder, but the police seal remained in place and no one made it inside the house.

That didn't mean Harper wasn't convinced that someone was there.

"I'm sorry about last night but ... I know I saw something."

Jared sipped his coffee at the kitchen table the next morning and kept his gaze speculative without being accusatory. "I know you did." He patted her hand on top of the table. "I'm not mad."

Harper wasn't sure she believed that. "You were out there in the cold for thirty minutes."

"Yes, and when I got back, I got to get warm with you. Why would I be angry about that?" Jared did his best to placate Harper, but he wasn't sure whether or not she believed his words.

"I'm still sorry." Harper scrubbed at the side of her face to wake up. "This is why I should always keep my ghost talks to myself. I knew that and I woke you anyway. It won't happen again."

Jared swiveled to face her, his eyes fiery. "That's not what I want."

His vehemence took Harper by surprise. "I ... what do you want?"

"I want you to share what you're feeling with me." Jared was firm. "If you happen to be feeling that a ghost is in the room and needs help, then I want to be part of that."

"But ... you didn't find anything and you missed out on sleep. You look tired this morning and it's all my fault."

"It's not your fault," Jared countered. "You look tired, too. Is that my fault?"

Harper shrugged. "You did want to do some aggressive cuddling when you came back."

Jared barked out a laugh, amused. "It's okay." He smoothed the back of her bed-mussed hair as he sobered. "Don't ever be sorry for waking me up because you think there might be someone outside at the neighbor's house. I'm not upset about being woken up, but I will be upset if you do something like that."

Harper stared at him for a long beat. "Right. Well ... thanks for looking."

"That's what strong protectors do," Zander said, his hair standing on end as he slid omelets in front of Harper and Jared. "Now ... eat up. I didn't wake up at the crack of dawn to cook so you guys could spend the entire morning gazing at each other and thinking 'no, you're prettier.'"

Jared choked on a bite of toast as he fought to recover from Zander's impression of him. "I'll keep that in mind." He swallowed hard. "Speaking of that, though, what are you guys going to do today?"

Harper held up her hands and shrugged. "I honestly have no idea. I don't think I've been much help on this one."

"On the contrary," Jared argued. "You're always helpful." He kissed the tip of her nose. "We're starting with Mike Dunlap. He's our best shot of getting answers. If he gives us anything, I'll give you a call."

Harper was hopeful. "Do you expect him to give you anything?"

"Probably not."

Harper's smile fled. "I honestly don't know what we're going to do. If Henry pops up and has answers, though, you're the first one I'll call."

"That sounds like a plan."

HARPER CAME UP WITH AN IDEA LESS THAN AN HOUR after Jared left for work. It was one Zander had absolutely zero interest in.

"Call me when you come up with something exciting," he suggested, settling on the couch with Shawn so they could watch some home improvement shows on HGTV. "Until then ... adios." He offered up a half wave but didn't turn from the television.

Harper knew she was on her own and she was fine with it.

She showered, changed, and headed toward Carol's house. She expected the single mother to answer the door when she knocked, but instead Marley stood there – a pair of flannel sleep pants and a T-shirt swallowing her enough that she looked three years younger than she was – and scowled.

"What are you doing here?"

Harper swallowed hard in the face of the girl's animosity. She thought she would have to work her way through Carol first. This change threw her for a loop.

"I came to visit you," Harper announced. It wasn't exactly a lie. Harper hoped to see Marley because Henry's funeral was later in the afternoon and Harper believed Carol probably kept her daughter out of school. She thought she would have to build up to it, though. "I wanted to see how you were feeling after being questioned by the cops last night."

"Oh, well, how sweet of you," Marley deadpanned, leaving Harper in the open door and stalking back inside the house. "Since your boyfriend is the one responsible for all of this, I'm betting you feel guilty."

"That's not the word I would use." Harper carefully shut the door and followed Marley into the kitchen. "Is there a reason I should feel guilty?"

"Well ... Mike called and broke up with me last night." Marley said the words as if they were accompanied by a natural disaster.

"Well, I hate to say it, but you're probably better off." Harper hoisted herself onto one of the counter stools and fixed Marley with a curious look as the girl filled the coffee machine and set it to percolate.

"Just out of curiosity, did he call before or after Jared and Mel stopped by his place to interview him?"

Marley made an exaggerated face only a mother could love ... and maybe not even then. "What do you think?"

"I think you have a bad attitude and I'm not exactly sure why," Harper answered honestly. "I know you think you have it rough – that's how all teenagers feel, after all – but you really have no idea how good you have it."

"Good?" Marley's eyebrows flew up her forehead. "I have it good? How do you figure that?"

"You have a roof over your head and a mother who loves you," Harper answered without hesitation. "What more do you want?"

"How about to be popular? How about to have a boyfriend who loves me? I don't think that's too much to ask."

Harper exhaled heavily as she rubbed the side of her temple. "Marley, I know you think popularity is the most important thing out there right now but it's not. That's a teenager thing. You're going to realize – hopefully sooner rather than later – that popularity means nothing. It's the true friends you surround yourself with that matter. Popularity is a high school construct and it goes away."

Marley blinked several times in rapid succession. "Did you see that on *Dr. Phil* or something?"

Harper scowled. "I learned it on my own."

"Let me guess ... you were unpopular in high school," Marley intoned. "Of course, you would have to be with that goofy friend of yours. By the way, how did such a hot guy end up gay? It's a total waste."

Harper bit her tongue to keep from exploding. "You don't know Zander and if you speak about him that way again, we're going to have a problem."

"Oh, well, la-di-da." Marley wrinkled her nose. "Why are you even here?"

"I wanted to check on you, although now that I'm here, I'm not sure why that is." Harper rolled her neck so she could stare at the ceiling. "I thought maybe your mother would be here and need some help."

"She's at the funeral home. Grandpa's service is today."

"I know." Harper flicked her eyes back to Marley. "How does that make you feel?"

"Oh, geez." Marley made an exaggerated face as she rolled her eyes so hard Harper was convinced she might fall over. "Are you my shrink now?"

"No, but I'm not convinced you couldn't use one." Harper refused to back down despite Marley's annoyance. "Are you really this upset about losing Mike Dunlap?"

"Of course I'm upset. He's the quarterback of the football team."

"So what?"

"So ... that means he's the most popular guy in the school," Marley explained. "When I was his girlfriend, that made me the most popular girl by default."

"And how did that work?"

"Are you slow or something?" Marley was belligerent. "I was the most popular girl in school. That means everyone wanted to hang out with me, be with me."

"And yet you got dumped by your boyfriend yesterday and are here alone on the day of your grandfather's funeral," Harper pointed out. "That doesn't strike me as real popularity."

"Oh, yeah? What would you know?"

"I know I wasn't popular in high school, like you said."

Marley sneered. "There's a news flash for you."

Harper managed to tamp down her temper, but just barely. "I also know I had the greatest friend who ever lived and I still have him today. Ask yourself something, Marley, who is here for you? All those friends you essentially paid for because you were trying to buy off Mike, where are they? I'm pretty sure they're gone because they were never really your friends."

"Do you think I care about that?" Marley's eyes filled with challenge. "I just wanted to be popular. I didn't care about making lifelong friends."

"Well, that's good, because there was no way that was going to happen given the way you were going about it." Harper sipped the coffee Marley absently shoved in front of her. "I'm curious what you think is going to happen now."

The conversational shift caught Marley off guard. "What do you mean?"

"Mike is being questioned by Jared and Mel this morning," Harper supplied. "I'm curious how you think that will go."

Marley shrugged, noncommittal. "I don't know. He'll probably just tell them he has no idea where that fertilizer came from and that will be it."

"Yeah, the thing is, that's the same fertilizer that killed your grandfather."

For the first time since Harper arrived on her doorstep, Marley looked shaken. "What?"

"That's the same fertilizer that killed your grandfather," Harper repeated, going for broke. "That fertilizer is rare because it was banned ten years ago. Anyone caught near it is going to be a suspect ... and Mike is the prime one right now."

Marley snorted, recovering. "Mike isn't a murderer. What would be his motivation?"

"To help you."

Marley stiffened. "Do you honestly think I killed my grandfather?"

Harper held her hands palms up. "I don't know. I want to believe that's not the case, but you're not exactly pleasant and I haven't seen you shed one tear for your grandfather."

"That's because he doesn't deserve any tears," Marley grumbled. "What do you want from me? Why are you really here?"

"I just wanted to see you before ... well, before things take a shift you're not expecting."

"And what shift would that be?"

"I don't know." Harper purposely kept her expression bland. "I'm just wondering what you think Mike will say when the heat comes down on him? I mean ... you were the one promising him gifts as soon as you got your inheritance. You are the one who showed no remorse over your grandfather's death. It seems clear he might choose a specific path."

Initially confused, Marley wrinkled her forehead. "I don't understand. In fact … ." Realization dawned very slowly, but when it did, the girl's face flooded with color. "You think he's going to tell the police I was the one who used the fertilizer to kill my grandfather, don't you?"

Harper adopted an innocent expression. "I didn't say that."

"But you think it, don't you?"

"I think you're in a rather rough position," Harper clarified. "I also think it might do you some good to talk about what you're feeling."

"With who?"

Harper arched an eyebrow.

"You?" Marley was incredulous. "Why would I possibly want to talk to you?"

"Because I don't see where you have a lot of options."

Marley heaved out a sigh, annoyed. "Fine. This doesn't mean I like you, though. Don't think that's what's going on here."

"Oh, don't worry. I don't like you either."

MIKE DUNLAP WAS A BALL OF NERVES WHEN HIS PARENTS let Jared and Mel into their house. He sat on the couch, his mother flanking him on one side while his uncle Don – who just happened to be a lawyer – sat on the other.

"I still don't think this is a good idea," Mike whined as he shifted uncomfortably. "On television they say you're never supposed to talk to the cops."

Mike's father, Barry Dunlap, growled as he shook his head. "You're going to tell them what you know or you're on your own."

Mike balked. "But … ."

"Listen to your father," Sally Dunlap ordered, glaring at her son. "We're both tired of this and want it to be over with."

Mike blew out a sigh that ruffled his bangs, his stomach rolling as he faced off with Jared and Mel. "Fine. What do you want to know?"

"For starters, we want to know if you have any reason to believe that Marley Winstead might have killed her grandfather," Mel started, opting not to mince words. "After you answer that question, we'll move on from there."

Mike squirmed. "I don't think Marley would kill her grandfather."

"You're not sure, though, are you?" Jared was grim. "What did she say to you?"

"Oh, I don't know if I should answer that." He looked to his mother for help but her expression was dark and pointed. "She said she wasn't sorry he was dead," he said finally. "She said he was always rude and mean to her and she was glad he was gone."

"How was he rude to her?" Jared asked.

"I don't know." Mike dragged a restless hand through his hair. "Can't we do this later? I'm not comfortable missing school. If the principal doesn't okay my absence, I won't be able to play in Friday's game."

"That's a total bummer," Jared deadpanned. "Perhaps you should focus on us and the questions we're asking so you're not so late it comes into play. How does that sound?"

"Like pure torture," Mike grumbled.

"Yes, we're looking forward to it, too," Jared drawled. "What things did Henry do to Marley?"

"He just told her stuff like girls were supposed to go to college and she would've been smarter if she were a boy," Mike replied. "You know ... stuff Marley already knew."

Jared made a face. "I don't know anything of the sort. That's not important, though. I want to know if you think Marley is capable of killing her grandfather."

"What?" Mike looked as if he'd rather be somewhere else – anywhere else, actually. "I don't know what you want me to say."

"Do you think Marley hated her grandfather enough to kill him?" Mel asked.

Mike looked to his mother and father for help, but they remained immobile. Ultimately he sucked in a breath and nodded. "I think she could've killed him. That's how much she hated him."

That was exactly what Jared was afraid of. "I see." He exchanged a quick look with Mel, something unsaid passing between them. "How did Marley get the fertilizer from the building at the school?"

Mike furrowed his brow. "What fertilizer?"

"I thought Henry was killed with arsenic," Don interjected.

Mel shook his head. "The arsenic poison panel dinged, but ultimately it was fertilizer that killed him ... a fertilizer that's been off the market for ten years, in fact."

Now it was Sally's turn to make a face. "But how would Marley get her hands on that?"

"There was some stored in the old building by the high school," Mel replied. "A bag of it was removed from the premises and moved to the spot beneath Jason Thurman's deck at the restaurant. That happens to be a spot where both Mike and Marley were seen hanging out."

Sally balked. "Our son didn't kill anyone."

"Of course he didn't," Mel said soothingly. "We still need to know how Marley got the fertilizer ... and even more importantly, how she got Henry to ingest it."

"I see." Sally made a tsking sound with her tongue. "What a mess." She glanced at her son. "Tell the detectives what you know. The faster you do it, the faster this will be over with."

"That's the thing," Mike hedged. "Marley never had anything to do with that fertilizer. She didn't so much as touch it as far as I know."

Jared didn't bother to hide his surprise. "So ... what was it doing there?"

Mike shrugged. "I didn't put it there."

"Do you know who did?"

"Yeah. It was Grandpa ... but it's not as if he's a killer or anything so I think you've screwed things up."

Jared was floored. "Excuse me?"

❧ 18 ❧

EIGHTEEN

"What do you mean your grandfather put it there?" Mel asked, resting his palms on his knees. "I'm not sure I understand."

"I'm not sure I understand either," Barry said, fixing his son with a steely-eyed glare. "Your grandfather is already in Florida for the year."

"Not *that* grandfather." Mike went back to shifting on his seat. "I was talking about my other grandfather."

Sally's eyes widened. "My father?"

Mike nodded. "He's the one who had the idea to grab the fertilizer. He knew where it was and everything."

"Wait a second." Jared held up his hands to still everyone. "I think I'm going to need more information."

"I think we're all going to need more information," Mel said, leaning back in his chair. "I think you should start from the beginning."

"I DON'T KNOW WHY YOU FELT THE NEED TO BRING me here."

Zander was bitter as Harper led him toward the front door of the senior center. Upon her return to the house after her visit with Marley, she spent twenty minutes pacing and then announced they were leaving. Zander, who was perfectly happy watching television all day, fought the effort ... and came up empty.

"We're here because this place depresses me and we have way too many Halloween decorations," Harper replied without hesitation, clutching a bag full of twinkle lights and a dancing skeleton to her chest. "I want to brighten up this place."

Zander stared at her for a long beat. "What are we really doing here?"

"I just told you."

"No, you're up to something else." Zander tapped his bottom lip with his finger. "What did Marley say to you?"

"Marley said ... ." Harper broke off, unsure how to answer.

"Did she admit to killing her grandfather?"

Harper immediately started shaking her head. "No. She claims she hated him and he was mean to her but she would never kill him."

"But?"

"I'm not sure I believe her, but I'm kind of leaning toward her telling the truth," Harper admitted. "The thing is, when she broke down completely and started talking, she was a normal kid going through everyday crap that she wasn't equipped to deal with. That doesn't make her a murderer."

"And here we go," Zander muttered, rubbing the back of his neck. "Harp, the kid is all sorts of messed up. She's mean, nasty, and she wears extremely ugly shoes. How can you possibly believe anything that comes out of her mouth?"

"I didn't say I believed her," Harper hedged. "I merely said ... I'm not sure."

"That still doesn't explain why we're here."

"I thought we could use our excess decorations to brighten the day of some senior citizens," Harper said evasively.

Zander wasn't falling for that for a second. "And?"

"And I also thought we might talk to Henry's friends – er, the people who occasionally allowed Henry to play cards with them – and get more information on the type of man he was and who might've targeted him for elimination."

"Oh, geez." Zander let loose with a rueful smile. "Trixie Belden is back on the case, huh?"

Harper shrugged. "It's bothering me. I can't shake it."

"Why? You didn't even like Henry."

"And I still don't. Marley is right about him being mean. He's mean ... and blunt ... and he doesn't care about other people's feelings."

"So why are you so determined to find answers on this?" Zander asked. "You could help him move over and let it go, but you're pushing ... and you're pushing hard."

"I don't know." It wasn't a lie. Harper honestly meant it. "It's as if there's a little voice inside of me and it's yelling that I'm close to figuring out the answer. You know how I love a good puzzle."

"I do," Zander confirmed. "You like a puzzle because if you don't focus on one thing your mind will scatter to the four winds. That's why you do actual puzzles for half the winter ... so you don't drive me crazy."

"So?"

"So I just have one question for you," Zander pressed. "Are you focusing on Henry because you don't want to focus on what we talked about before?"

Harper conveniently averted her gaze. "I can't remember what we talked about before."

"Oh, don't do that." Zander shook his head, disdain practically dripping from his tongue. "We both talked and agreed that, once this is over, we're going to sit down with Shawn and Jared and have a talk about what's to come."

"Oh, *that*." Harper pasted a big smile on her face. "I thought a bit more about that and have decided I'm going to let you do it."

"Do what?"

"Talk to Jared and Shawn. I think the conversation should be a man thing."

Zander snagged the back of Harper's hoodie before she could disappear inside of the senior center. "Excuse me?"

"You heard me." Harper's smile dipped. "I want you to talk to Jared and Shawn and then report back to me."

"Since when are you a big baby when it comes to relationship stuff?"

"Since the idea of talking about this with Jared makes me want to puke," Harper replied, not missing a beat. "It's not going to end well. I can feel it."

Zander released her hoodie but kept a hand on her shoulder in case she decided to bolt. "Why don't you think it will end well?"

"Because it can't possibly end well," Harper answered. "Let's say I bring it up and he looks at me as if I have two heads. I can't take it back. Once that suggestion is out there, it can't be stuffed back inside the bottle."

"He's not going to look at you as if you have two heads."

"You can't possibly know that."

"Oh, I know it." Zander offered up a small headshake as he stared at a spot on the wall over Harper's shoulder. "I promise you that he'll be open to the suggestion."

Harper was suddenly suspicious. "What do you know?"

Zander balked. "I don't know anything. I believe you're already aware of that, though."

Harper narrowed her eyes. "No, you know something. I want to know what it is."

Zander dropped his hand from Harper's shoulder and focused on the door. "We should totally go inside and start decorating. It's probably going to take us hours to work through all the stuff that we brought."

Harper wasn't about to fall for her best friend's bad acting attempt. "What do you know?"

"I know that you're very pretty and I have several ideas for group costumes," Zander replied, sliding around Harper and grabbing the door. "How do you feel about *The Golden Girls?*"

"Oh, I'm not going to let it go that easily," she announced.

"I have no idea what you're talking about." Zander was breezy as he stepped into the senior center. "By the way, I'm totally going to be Blanche. I think you should be Rose."

"Start running now," Harper ordered. "I'm not letting you off the hook."

"I was afraid you were going to say that."

"I DON'T KNOW HOW IT STARTED." MIKE WAS SO NERVOUS he couldn't stop rubbing his hands over his knees in an effort to wipe away the sweat. "I guess it started when I went with Marley to the senior center one day."

"And why would you go there?" Sally challenged. "You've never shown any interest in hanging out with your grandfather before."

"And, trust me, if I had a choice I wouldn't go back there again," Mike said. "It's a depressing place and it smells like that stuff Dad rubs on his back after he golfs."

"That's a muscle relaxation thing," Barry said, wrinkling his nose. "That's for people my age ... not old people."

Mike rolled his eyes. "Whatever. Anyway, Marley insisted we stop in because she was dropping off something for her grandfather. She was always sucking up to him."

"But why?" Jared asked, legitimately curious. "Why would Marley go out of her way for Henry given the fact that they had such a rocky relationship?"

"That's exactly why I think she did it. She always complained that he was rude and mean and yet she ran around town and did errands for him all the time."

"Did you ever ask her why?"

Mike nodded. "That's when she told me about the inheritance."

"What inheritance?" Don asked.

"Marley's grandfather promised he was going to leave her a lot of money so she could either buy a house or go to school when he died," Mike explained. "I thought he was blowing smoke up her ... you know ... but she was convinced he was telling the truth because he always told the truth, even when it was cruel."

"Ah." Jared thought he understood. "I guess that makes sense. Henry made a name for himself by being blunt so Marley assumed everything he told her — whether good or bad — was the truth. That explains that."

"That doesn't explain about the fertilizer," Mel pressed.

"I'm getting to that." Mike's eyes flashed. "Anyway, she insisted on going to the senior center and taking her grandfather things like lunch and snacks ... and one time she took him hemorrhoid cream, but we agreed to never speak of that. One day when we were up there, I realized her grandfather was playing cards with my grandfather."

"I didn't get the feeling that Dad even liked Henry," Sally noted, wrinkling her nose. "In fact, I thought he downright hated him."

"I think most people in town tended to dislike Henry because of what he did for a living," Mel supplied. "He was code enforcement and he got overzealous at times."

"Right." Sally nodded her head in understanding. "That's right. I'd almost forgotten about that."

Jared found his interest piqued. "Forgotten about what?"

"Dad got ticketed by Henry once for having a boat in the front yard," Sally explained. "He saved up forever for that boat, but it was delivered early and he didn't have a place to store it for a week. He thought he would get away with it because he talked to all the neighbors, but either someone complained or Henry noticed while driving by."

"Oh, this is sparking something in my memory," Mel noted. "Henry ticketed the boat and your father told him to stuff it. Henry came back every day and added more tickets and your father refused to pay them. Eventually a warrant was issued for your father's arrest because of the tickets and it became a huge thing."

"That's essentially it," Sally confirmed. "Dad was spitting mad and he actually got on the township agenda over it. He was there — and so was Henry — and they started screaming at one another in front of everyone. It was so embarrassing."

Jared was flummoxed. "And all of this was over a few nuisance tickets?"

"That's what they said, but I always thought it was more than that," Barry offered." I even asked my father-in-law what the deal was one day, but he said it was too long of a story to tell and it wasn't important. He said all that was important was that Henry was a liar and that he wasn't nearly as proper as he pretended to be."

"Proper?" Mel's eyebrow migrated north. "That's an odd word to use."

"I don't think you understand," Sally said. "It didn't stop with the boat incident. After the city council rescinded the tickets for the boat, Henry started stopping by once a week to issue tickets. It was ... ridiculous. Each ticket he wrote drove my father further around the bend.

"My mother tried to talk my father down – this was long before she died, of course – but he always seemed just as angry at her as he was at Henry when she tried to stop them from fighting," she continued. "The only reason it stopped is because Henry stopped working for the city."

"Yeah, and I heard Henry was forced into retirement before he was ready because of that stupid war," Barry added. "Henry filled in for sick workers for years after he retired and he came back each and every time and wrote a ticket for my father-in-law."

Mel was naturally perturbed. "I only remember parts of this story. I can't say as I've ever heard all of it."

"I think the town council wanted to keep it on the down low," Barry said. "It made everybody look bad."

"It certainly did," Mel agreed. "That doesn't explain the fertilizer, though."

"Oh, right." Mike forced his eyes from the clock on the wall. "I ran into Grandpa one day and he was playing cards with Mr. Spencer. I thought it was weird because of all the fights they had so I asked him about it.

"He didn't say much at first and just said he was over it, even though I didn't believe him," he continued. "I didn't think anything about it until a month later when he caught me as I was leaving the parking lot and told me he needed me to run an errand for him."

"What errand?" Jared asked.

"He took me to that old building by the high school and told me to load up a bag of fertilizer."

"Did you?"

"Well, yeah." Mike shrugged. "I didn't see what the big deal was. He worked as a janitor for the school for years and he said he left that fertilizer in that building and the principal said he could take it for personal use. I honestly didn't think it was a thing."

"Okay, but that doesn't explain how it ended up underneath the restaurant deck," Jared pressed.

"That happened two days ago," Mike supplied. "Grandpa called and said he didn't need the fertilizer any longer and that I should get rid of it. I said I didn't know where to get rid of it – I didn't think it was something I could just dump in the trash – and asked why he couldn't handle it himself.

"He said he had other things to do and the bag was too heavy so I had to do it," he continued. "I was sick of arguing about it so I picked up the bag and asked where I should put it. He got irritated and said I should hide it under the restaurant because no one would look under there until spring due to the weather. He said we might get lucky and the water would take care of it."

"And you didn't find anything odd about that?" Mel asked.

Mike shrugged. "Not really. Grandpa is old. He says odd things all the time. He also trims his nose hair when I'm sitting right in front of him. He's an odd dude. I don't know what you want me to say."

Jared and Mel exchanged a weighted look.

"You think it was Dad, don't you?" Sally's face drained of color as she regarded the two police officers.

"I think there's a definite possibility that your father might've been involved," Mel admitted. "It never sat right with me for Marley to be the prime suspect. She's a pain the butt and everything, but she's still just a kid and her motive was tenuous."

"But ... she wanted money," Sally said. "Her motive is worse than my father's motive."

"She wasn't in Henry's will, though. He was playing her," Jared explained. "It's true that Marley didn't know that, but it's also true she doesn't exactly look like a killer. She's a kid, for crying out loud."

"I've heard plenty of stories about kids killing people for no good reason," Barry argued.

"I have, too," Mel said, getting to his feet. "We're not ruling her out. Until then, though, we need to talk to your father."

"Because you think he's a murder suspect?" Sally was beside herself.

"I think he's as good a suspect as anyone at this point, and right now I simply want to talk to him," Mel replied. "That doesn't mean I think he's guilty."

"Well ... I'm calling an attorney for him." Sally headed toward the kitchen. "I'm calling one right now."

"I'm your lawyer," Don called out.

"I want a better lawyer than you for my father."

"Oh, but he was okay for me," Mike complained. "That's great, Mom."

"Shut up, Michael. I've had enough of you for one day," Sally barked. "This is all your fault."

Jared fought to maintain his temper as he focused on Barry. "Where would your father be right now?"

"Either home or at the senior center. Those are really the only two options."

"Thanks. We'll be in touch."

19

NINETEEN

"**W**hat are you guys doing back?"

Annie stopped at the refreshment table when she caught sight of Harper and Zander, her expression quizzical.

"Harper is torturing me," Zander replied.

"Why?"

"I think she likes it."

Harper shot Zander a quelling look. "We bought far too many decorations and decided to bring the extras here so you guys could enjoy them."

Annie smirked. "Don't you think we're a bit old for decorations?"

"You're young at heart, aren't you?"

Annie shrugged. "I guess. It seems a bit much, though."

"I don't know," Zander said, changing course. "I saw a flier and you guys are having a Halloween party in a few weeks. That sounds fun."

"I think you need to look up the definition of 'fun,'" Annie said. "Our Halloween party is simply a way for some people to spike the orange punch and others to dress up like morons."

"Hey, I happen to like dressing up," Zander argued. "We were just talking about a group costume for this year. I suggested we dress up like *The Golden Girls*."

"And I quickly vetoed that because there's no way that Jared and Shawn are going to dress up like women."

"Iconic women."

"It doesn't matter."

"You're absolutely no fun," Zander groused as he pulled out a box of twinkle lights. "What if we dress up like *The Flintstones*. You can be Wilma – which means Jared will be Fred – and I can be Betty because I look good in blue."

Harper furrowed her brow. "I don't see Jared going for that either."

"Fine. What do you think we should dress up as? And, keep in mind, it has to be a famous foursome."

"Well ... ." Harper racked her brain. "What about the Fantastic Four? I can be the Invisible Woman. Jared can be Mr. Fantastic. Shawn can be the Human Torch."

"And what does that leave me?"

"You can be that big boulder dude."

Zander was affronted. "Absolutely not! I want a costume that shows off how handsome I am. Granted, I can be handsome in any costume, but I draw the line at being a human rock."

"Fine. Pick something else."

"You guys are a trip," Annie noted, taking the open chair by the end of the table and sipping her coffee. "You're better than cards and television."

"You've got that right," Zander readily agreed. "As for costumes ... how about Veronica and the Heathers from *Heathers*."

"No. That's four women again."

"You're being awful stingy with the rules."

"You have to pick something where Jared and Shawn can be guys," Harper argued. "Like ... what about the *Teenage Mutant Ninja Turtles*?"

Zander shot his best friend a withering look. "Be serious."

"I am being serious."

"No, you're not. How about the leads in *Sisterhood of the Traveling Pants*? Or, even better. How about the four leads in *Mean Girls*?"

Harper narrowed her eyes. "I'm going to stop talking about this if you don't pick something realistic."

"I don't see you coming up with famous foursomes that will work."

"Okay, well ... how about the kids from *South Park*?"

"No."

"*Scooby-Doo*? We could borrow someone's dog."

"Who gets to be Daphne?"

"Me."

"No."

"*The Four Musketeers*? Oh, how about The Beatles? You love sixties fashion."

Zander shifted from one foot to the other. "*The Four Musketeers* are out. You know how I feel about feathers."

"I'm sorry." Harper held up her hands in mock surrender. "I didn't think about the feathers in their caps."

"The Beatles is something we can discuss later, although I'm not completely sold."

"Okay. At least we're getting somewhere. How about *The Wizard of Oz*? I can be Dorothy and you can be the Scarecrow. You love that movie."

"I do love that movie." Zander pursed his lips. "Do you really think we can get Shawn and Jared into the other two costumes?"

"Probably not."

"Then why suggest it?"

"Because I need to focus on costumes rather than the secret you're keeping from me," Harper shot back.

Zander straightened. "Right. I bet I can get Shawn to dress up as the Cowardly Lion. That only leaves you to get Jared to dress up as the Tin Man."

"He's probably not going to do it."

"We could make him one of the witches."

"Nothing with a dress," Harper barked. "I mean ... why can't you get that through your head?"

"Because it severely limits our options."

"I think you guys are missing the obvious choice," Annie interjected. "It's sitting right in front of you and you've totally glossed over it."

"*The Goonies?*" Harper asked.

"Oh, that's a good idea." Zander perked up. "We don't have enough people, though. By the way, if we do that, I'm Brand."

"As long as I'm Data, I don't care."

"Should we make Jared be Chunk or Mouth?"

"Good question."

"Ooh, or Sloth."

"Or how about *Ghostbusters?*" Annie suggested, quickly growing weary of the conversation. "You guys work with ghosts in real life, right? Doesn't it make sense for you guys to use that to your advantage when picking costumes?"

Harper stilled, dumbfounded. "Huh."

"That's not a bad idea," Zander said after a beat. "It allows us to carry around fake ray guns and shoot people with slime. Why didn't we think of that?"

"Probably because we're idiots." Harper tilted her head to the side, considering. "I think I could talk Jared into that costume."

"I think I could talk Shawn into it, too."

"See, it's all settled." Annie beamed. "Now that you're not arguing about that, what can you tell me about Henry? His death is still the talk of the senior center and we're all anxious to hear what you know."

"All?" Zander asked.

"All," Annie confirmed, gesturing for Glenn, Eve, and Carl to join her. The three friends ambled over without further prodding. "We want to know what you know."

"Well, it's kind of a long story," Harper hedged.

"We love long stories," Glenn said, grabbing a chair. "We especially like it when pretty women tell them."

Harper extended a warning finger. "I'll hurt you again if you're not careful."

"I promise to behave myself."

"Okay, well ... I don't see why not."

"HE'S NOT HERE."

Jared covered his eyes to blot out the sun as he stared into the non-descript ranch house. The front bay window was open and allowed a view of everything.

"Technically we have no reason to go inside," Mel hedged. "We don't have probable cause."

"You're right." Jared licked his lips. "The thing is, I think I heard someone crying for help."

"You did?" Mel didn't immediately grasp Jared's investigative tactic suggestion. "I didn't hear anything." He pressed his ear to the window and waited. "Seriously, I don't hear anything ... and his car isn't in the driveway."

Jared exhaled heavily. Apparently he was going to have to spell things out for his partner, something he wasn't keen to do. "I did. You know, he's an old guy. He might have fallen and broken a hip. That sound I heard could've been his last gasp before he lost consciousness."

"But ... his car isn't here."

"No. It could be at the shop."

"I think you just want a reason to go in and take a look around," Mel groused.

Jared folded his arms over his chest and waited.

"Oh." Realization dawned on Mel.

"There it is." Jared's smile was mischievous. "The thing is, do you think you heard a noise inside?"

"Let me listen again." Mel made a big show of resting his head against the window. "Yup. I heard something. We should probably go inside to make sure that he's okay."

"That's exactly what I was thinking."

"SO IT WASN'T ARSENIC?" Eve made a clucking sound as she shook her head. "I didn't see that coming."

"No one did," Harper said. "It seems that the arsenic panel alerted so they knew it was poison, but it took further tests to drill down."

"And do they know where the poison came from?" Carl asked.

"Perhaps it came from someone's poisoned lips," Glenn suggested, waggling his eyebrows. "I would love to get a poison kiss."

Annie shot him a dubious look. "Even if you die from it?"

Glenn shrugged. "Sometimes a kiss is worth it."

"Whatever." Annie rolled her eyes. "So, do the cops think Marley did it? I know that's the way they were looking because of the questions you asked."

Harper had no idea how much she should share, but she liked the group – especially Annie – and saw no reason to lie. "I don't know that they've ruled out Marley, but I saw her this morning and I can't say I believe she's a killer."

"Who else would it be?" Carl asked. "Marley was the one who thought she was going to get an inheritance."

"Yeah, but that doesn't mean she's a killer," Harper said. "I know they're questioning her boyfriend this morning because they believe he might have some important answers."

"Who is her boyfriend?" Eve asked, confused. "I think I should know but ... oh, wait. It's Mike Dunlap." She shifted so she faced Carl. "He's your grandson, isn't he?"

A muscle worked in Carl's jaw as he nodded. "Yes."

"You should probably call over there," Annie instructed. "If your grandson is a suspect, that's going to mean a lot of upheaval in the family."

"I'm sure he's not a suspect," Carl said, his eyes dark as they landed on Harper's face. "He's not, right?"

Harper shrugged. "I honestly have no idea. That fertilizer bag was big. I doubt very much Marley could carry it on her own. She needed help."

"But ... ." Carl shifted on his chair. "Maybe I should call home."

"It probably couldn't hurt." Harper was distracted by the lights Zander insisted on hanging in a spider web pattern. "Don't you think that's a bit much?"

"Don't mess with the master," Zander shot back.

"Fine. I'm going to run to the storage closet and see if I can find some tape. We're going to need more than we brought."

"Yeah. You get on that."

"HE'S NOT HERE," MEL ANNOUNCED, WANDERING INTO Carl's office and pulling up short when he found Jared studying a tapestry of photographs and paper taped to the small room's wall. "What is that?"

"I think it's a motive for murder," Jared replied, his eyes busy. "I mean ... he's set up a timeline here."

"What do you mean?" Mel migrated to Jared's side so he could study the wall. "Oh, I see what you're getting at. He even put the first citation up on the wall over here." He pointed. "Good grief. There have to be a hundred citations tacked up here."

"Yeah, I'm thinking Henry was a bit of a control freak or something." Jared moved his eyes to a photo in the middle of the spread. "Do you know who that woman is?"

Mel nodded. "It's Cathy. That's Carl's wife. She died about a year ago."

"How?"

"She was in an assisted living center for two years before she died. Some people said she had Alzheimer's. Others said she had dementia. I'm not quite sure. I know that she got so bad Carl had no choice but to move her into a home, which she didn't take well."

"How do you know that?"

"She put up a fight when it came time to go, spouting some hateful stuff," Mel replied. "The neighbors called because Carl was having trouble controlling her so I helped him load her up and followed him to the home. This was long before you got here."

"Did Carl visit her in the home?"

"Oh, yeah, he was dedicated even though I understand she couldn't even remember him after she was there for six months." Mel's expression was sympathetic. "I would rather die at eighty with all my faculties than eighty-five with no memory of who I was or those I left behind."

Jared nodded, understanding. "Yeah. Me, too. I still don't understand why she's on this board. Did Henry write tickets for her, too?"

"I have no idea." Mel shuffled closer. "Let me look."

"I'll look over here." Jared shifted toward the desk. "We might find something useful."

"You know we're in a precarious position here," Mel pointed out. "We didn't exactly gain entry through legal means."

"Yeah, but Carl is in his eighties and he's not going to a regular prison anyway. He's too old. He'll probably get off on house arrest or shoved in a hospital."

Mel balked. "We don't know he's guilty."

"No," Jared agreed, picking up a stack of letters. "The thing is, it's looking more and more likely that it's him. He's clearly obsessed with Henry and he's the one who had Mike pick up the fertilizer. That's more than we've got on Marley."

"I know. It's just ... who kills someone over citations?"

Jared didn't immediately answer, his attention fully focused on the letters.

"Are you even listening to me?" Mel prodded, annoyance evident. "I'm talking here."

"Huh?" Jared ripped his attention away from the stack. "Yeah. I'm listening to you. It's just ... I think I found something."

"You think?" Mel moved away from the garish wall display.

"I know," Jared corrected. "Look at these." He handed the letters over to Mel and watched as the man flipped through them.

"They look like old correspondence," Mel said after a beat. "It looks as if someone was writing to Cathy."

"Read the top letter."

"Why? Cathy is long gone. She's clearly not part of this."

"I don't think that's true."

"Well ... ." Mel licked his lips as he dove into the letter, widening his eyes when he realized what he was looking at. "Oh, holy ... is this what I think it is?"

"It seems Cathy was having an affair," Jared noted. "Those letters are dated from the eighties but they're out in the open, which means Carl has been reading them. Did you see who they're from?"

Mel nodded, his mouth dry. "Henry. Cathy had an affair with Henry in the eighties. I still don't understand how that adds up to murder today."

"I think the answer is in the information you shared with me," Jared supplied. "You said Cathy and Carl were happy and he didn't want to put her in a home but had no choice. That was three years ago. You said he was devoted even after her memory completely disappeared."

"He was. I had an aunt at that facility and I swear Carl stopped in there every day."

"So he probably had hope that there would be a miracle or something," Jared said. "You said she died a year ago."

"So?"

"So maybe Carl waited until she died to start sorting through her stuff."

Things finally clicked into place for Mel. "And when he sorted through her stuff, he found the letters hidden away. He already hated Henry, although not enough to kill him. The letters changed things. He was grieving and needed someone to hate."

"And Henry fit that bill," Jared confirmed. "We need to get to that senior center and talk to Carl."

"I'm right there with you."

HARPER SEARCHED THE STORAGE CLOSET TWICE AND came up empty.

"No tape," she muttered to herself, annoyed. "How can they not have tape? Everyone knows you always need tape."

She didn't mind talking to herself as she searched. It somehow made the dingy small space more palatable. The room was technically larger than a closet but smaller than a bedroom. Harper moved to the other side of the storage rack and searched the shelves for tape. She was so lost in thought she almost didn't hear the door open.

"Do you need help?"

Harper recognized Carl's voice. "Oh, well, I don't think they have what I'm looking for."

"And what is that?"

"Tape."

"Well, I hardly think that's your biggest concern."

"What?" Harper dragged her eyes from the shelves and focused on Carl, widening her eyes when she saw the knife in his hand – something she was pretty sure he stole from the refreshment table – and the look of absolute hatred on his face. "Oh, well, crap. I didn't see this coming."

"I know. That's going to make things easier."

TWENTY

"What are you doing?"

Harper had trouble wrapping her head around what was happening.

"I'm here to ask you a few questions," Carl said, calmly walking around the edge of the shelf and pinning Harper with a pointed look. "I need to know exactly what your boyfriend knows."

"I think I can say with absolute certainty that I have no idea what Jared knows." This was hardly the first dangerous situation Harper found herself in and yet it felt somehow dire. There was only one exit door and the room was small. Since the shelf was wide and tall, it cut down her avenues of escape significantly. "He doesn't tell me about his cases."

"Oh, who are you trying to kid?" Carl made a disgusted face. "You just spent twenty minutes telling us exactly what you know ... and how you know it. Do you expect me to believe that?"

"I know what he knew last night," Harper clarified. "I have no idea what he's discovered this morning."

"And yet you know he's questioning my grandson," Carl mused. "I should've realized this would happen. I should've planned better."

Harper was convinced he was speaking to himself at the end, but she decided to take advantage of the situation and get answers – while also buying time to figure a way out of this mess. If she got lucky, Zander would come looking for her. She didn't want Zander to get hurt, but he was young and fit. The odds of Carl being able to get the drop on him – especially if there were two of them doing the fighting – were slim. She simply had to hold out until Zander figured out she was missing.

How long could that possibly be, even for someone as self-absorbed as Zander?

"I don't understand why you did it," Harper started, choosing her words carefully. "Is it because Henry was a mean old coot?"

"He was definitely that. That's not why I killed him, though."

"Did he write you citations when he was with code enforcement?"

"More than a hundred."

"A hundred?" Harper's eyes bugged out. "I ... what could you have possibly done that warranted a hundred citations?"

"I always wondered about that myself. It started with a boat and grew from there. I was angry about the boat citations, there's no getting around that, but I fought them and won. He wrote me up so many times his supervisor started tossing them the minute they passed over his desk."

"So ... why kill him now? He hasn't been with code enforcement for years."

"Technically, that's not true," Carl countered. "He was strongly urged to retire before he was ready because of his troubles with me. That made him unhappy, but they threw him a bone and said he could fill in when someone had a vacation or illness. That meant he filled in at least three times a year, usually more. Do you know who he came straight after whenever he was called to duty?"

"I'm going to guess you," Harper said dryly. "If the supervisor knew about your issues, though, why did it matter? The citations were dismissed. Henry was nothing more than a nuisance."

"That's what I thought until Cathy."

Harper was at a loss. "Cathy? Your wife?"

Carl nodded. "The love of my life."

Harper searched her memory. "She died about a year ago, right?"

"Only after spending two years in that hole I had to send her to." Carl was understandably bitter. "She hated that place."

"I understand that. I would hate that place, too. Still ... she was bad from what I understand. You couldn't possibly have taken care of her on your own. That's too much for one person to bear."

"I promised her when we got married that I would never put her in a place like that. I broke that promise."

"But ... you couldn't have foreseen what would happen in your eighties when you were making promises in your twenties," Harper pointed out. "I'm sure she understood."

"She didn't understand. She knew what was happening. In fact, while she still had her faculties, she made sure she hurt me as badly as I hurt her on the day she was taken away."

Harper had no idea what Cathy's mental health had to do with Henry's murder. Since Carl seemed keen to talk about it, though, she opted to play it out. "How?"

"She told me she had an affair."

Harper's heart rolled. "With Henry?"

"That's what she said, but I didn't believe her at first." Carl adopted a wistful expression. "I didn't believe her because she was so upset about being in the hospital that I thought she was lashing out. I pushed it out of my mind."

"But somehow you found out it was true, huh? Did she tell you again when she didn't know who she was?"

"No, but there were times I got the impression she thought she was talking to someone else," Carl replied. "She mentioned picnics we never took ... and a trip to Traverse City that I know I wasn't part of. I assumed it was her mind playing tricks on her and let it be.

"The last six months of her life were terrible," he continued. "She stopped talking completely by then and rolled into a ball on her bed, never moving. It was as if she forgot how to live. That's how it seemed to me, anyway.

"I still went every single day to see her," he said. "I read to her. Sometimes I just sat and held her hand. I wanted to be there when ... well, when it happened."

Harper swallowed hard. Even though she knew the man standing in front of her was a murderer, that didn't stop her from feeling sympathy. "I'm sorry."

"In the end, her body forgot how to breathe and she slipped away," Carl said. "It was both a relief and a curse. Do you understand that?"

Harper nodded without hesitation. "It was a relief because she was no longer suffering. It was a curse because the woman you loved was gone and you no longer had hope that she would miraculously recover."

"I know you probably think I'm stupid, but I did hope she would recover for two full years," Carl admitted. "Then, the moment she stopped breathing, the first thing I felt was release. I knew I wouldn't come to visit the following day, and I felt ... lighter."

"And that made you feel guilty," Harper surmised. "That still doesn't explain what happened with Henry."

"I'm getting to it." Carl murdered Harper with a dark glare. "I spent six months trying to figure out what to do with my days. Eventually that included coming here. I hated it at first, but Eve and Annie took me under their wings and I learned to tolerate Glenn and all his perverted talk."

"You're stronger than I am on that front."

Carl ignored the lame joke. "Then, one day, I decided to start sorting through Cathy's things. I knew it was time to put her to rest. She wouldn't want me to stop living even though she was no longer around to share a life with."

"That's probably true."

"I found the letters in her underwear drawer. They were packed away at the back and I almost missed them."

"What kind of letters?"

"Love letters. I didn't believe them at first – I actually thought Henry had somehow managed to sneak into my house and hide them when I wasn't looking – but the more I read, the more I realized they were true."

"So Cathy and Henry had an affair?" Harper searched her memory of the man in question. "That doesn't seem like him."

"According to the letters it went on for exactly six months," Carl explained. "I was traveling at the time – I was trying to be a truck driver rather than a janitor so we could have more money – and apparently Cathy got lonely."

"Well ... ." Harper wasn't sure what to say. "They didn't keep it up after that. They obviously realized it was wrong."

"They did. Cathy ended it. Henry kept writing after, though. He wouldn't give up. I'm convinced he only came to write me citations because he was bitter Cathy decided to stay with me."

In an odd way, that made sense to Harper. "So you decided to kill Henry because he slept with your wife forty years ago?"

"No, I decided to kill Henry because he tainted every moment of my marriage with his lies and deceit," Carl corrected. "He had it coming. I just wish he was still around so I could confront him about what he did with my wife. I want to hear what he has to say for himself ... the foul bastard."

As if on cue, Henry popped into view on the other side of the shelf and made Harper's heart sink.

"I told you it was assassins. He planned it from the start."

"Oh, well, great," Harper gritted out. "This is just ... un-freaking-believable."

JARED WAS STUNNED TO FIND ZANDER HOLDING COURT IN the middle of the senior center when he arrived. Mel scanned the room for signs of Carl, shaking his head when he came up empty.

"I don't see him."

Jared strode toward Zander, snagging the gregarious man's gaze. "What are you doing here?"

Zander didn't like Jared's tone. "Bringing joy and happiness to the world."

"Is he ever," Eve said, giggling.

Jared ignored the members of Zander's fan club. "Where is Harper? Is she here with you?"

"She is. She went to get some tape from the storage room."

"Now that you bring it up, she's been gone a long time," Annie noted.

Jared's inner danger alarm began alerting. "How long?"

187

"I don't know. At least thirty minutes."

"Where is Carl Hill?" Mel asked. "His car is in the parking lot, but I can't seem to find him."

"Oh, he's around." Annie airily waved her hand. "He heard you guys were questioning his grandson and had a meltdown of sorts. I think he's worried about the boy."

"No, he's not worried about his grandson," Jared gritted out. "Where is this storage closet?"

"In the back." Zander didn't pick up on Jared's worry. "I'm sure she'll be back in a minute."

Jared roughly grabbed Zander's elbow. "Where?"

Annoyance flashed in Zander's eyes, which was quickly replaced with worry. "Right over there. What's going on?"

Jared released Zander and stalked in the direction of the closet.

"What's going on?" Zander repeated.

"It's not good," Mel answered. "It's not good at all."

"DID YOU SLEEP with Cathy Hill, Henry?"

Harper didn't bother hiding her annoyance when Henry flashed her a sheepish look.

"You did, didn't you? Ugh. And I thought you were a jerk before I heard this part."

"What do you want me to say?" Henry challenged. "It was a mistake. We both knew it was a mistake. That's why we ended it."

"Yes, but you kept citing Carl for stupid crap even after you slept with his wife," Harper argued. "You gave him more than a hundred citations. Don't you think that's a bit excessive?"

Henry shrugged, noncommittal. "His lawn was always overgrown and his bushes were uneven."

"Oh, you're a freaking piece of work, aren't you?" Harper heaved out a disgusted sigh. "No wonder he killed you."

"Hey!" Henry was beside himself. "I slept with his wife like forty years ago. She's gone. That's no reason to kill me now."

"Did you keep giving him citations after you retired?"

"His yard was a mess!"

Harper slapped her hand to her forehead. "I can't even ... ."

"Who are you talking to?" Carl asked, curiously glancing around. "Are you losing your mind?"

"Sometimes that's exactly how it feels. I'm talking to Henry."

"Henry who?"

"Henry Spencer."

"But ... he's dead."

"He's not too quick on the draw, is he?" Henry made a tsking sound as he shook his head. "He should know I'm dead. He killed me."

"I thought you said it was assassins," Harper challenged.

"He is an assassin. He infiltrated our town and purposely didn't follow landscaping rules because he's a spy."

Harper held up her hand, disgusted. "Stop talking to me. You're a freak."

"Says the woman talking to a ghost," Henry muttered.

"I wish I couldn't talk to ghosts right now."

Carl's eyes widened with disbelief. "Are you trying to say those rumors about you are true?"

"You'll have to be more specific," Harper replied. "If you're talking about the rumors that I can talk to ghosts, yes, those are true. If you're talking about the rumor I have three boyfriends that Henry started spreading, no, that's not true.

Carl's mouth dropped open. "You have to be kidding me."

"I'm not kidding you."

"But ... you can't talk to ghosts," Carl pressed. "It's impossible."

"Anything is possible."

"I don't believe you."

"I can't really help that right now." Harper focused her eyes on the knife. "You know, Carl, I didn't do anything to you. I don't believe you really want to kill me. Why don't you put the knife down?"

"What? Oh, I can't." Carl tightened his grip on the weapon. "You know what I did."

"So does Jared by now. That's why you're so afraid. Killing me isn't going to help you in the long run."

"But ... I need time to get away." Carl regrouped. "Do you think you can talk to Cathy? I have a few questions and ... if you can talk to Henry, surely you can talk to Cathy."

Harper considered lying, but it seemed somehow cruel. "I don't think Cathy stayed behind. I think she was at peace when she died, especially after what you told me. I don't think you're going to be able to see Cathy until you cross over, too."

Tears flooded Carl's eyes. "But why did Henry get to stay?"

"My guess is because he's a fussy meanie who didn't like the idea of anyone else telling him what to do. I don't have an answer for you."

"But ... I want to talk to her."

Carl was so morose Harper could feel nothing but pity. "Someday," she said. "It's not today, though." She gestured with her hand. "I know you don't want to hurt me. Henry did you wrong and you made him pay. You don't want to do the same to me."

Carl was indecisive as he stared at the knife. "I don't want to go to jail."

"We'll see what we can figure out."

"Can you keep me out of jail?"

Harper opted for honesty. "I don't know. I guess we'll have to wait and see."

Carl licked his lips, dragging things out for what felt like forever, and then he handed over the knife. "I didn't want to hurt you anyway. You seem like a good girl – despite having three boyfriends, that is."

Harper forced a smile as the closet door sprung open and Jared rushed inside. "I only have one boyfriend."

"It's better that way," Carl said. "It's better to only love one person."

"I think it's good to love a lot of people," Harper countered. "I think you're right about big love, though. That should only be for one person."

Jared's eyes flashed as he glanced between faces. "Are you okay?"

"I'm fine." Harper kept hold of the knife. "Carl and I had a long talk. He's a little upset, but he doesn't want to hurt anyone."

"That's good," Mel said, striding into the room and drawing a set of cuffs from his belt. "I think everyone has been hurt enough in this case."

"Definitely," Jared agreed, claiming the knife from Harper's hand and pulling her in for a hug. "I was worried."

"This time it really wasn't my fault."

Jared chuckled as he kissed her forehead. "You are a magnet at times, aren't you?"

Harper shrugged. "This time it was more sad than anything else."

"I can live with that." Jared rested his cheek against her forehead. "You're still going to get a lecture."

"I figured."

Zander picked that moment to poke his head into the storage room, barely sparing a glance for Carl as Mel read the distraught man his rights and instead focusing on Harper. "Did you tell Jared we're going to be the Ghostbusters for Halloween?"

"I haven't gotten that far yet."

"Well, hurry along. We need to start planning now."

"I'll get right on it."

TWENTY-ONE

"Why are we over here?"

Two days later, life was back to normal ... for the most part. Zander managed to refrain from early morning bedroom visits – although the complaints were legendary – and Carl was in a local hospital undergoing a psychological evaluation.

He admitted to everything, including sneaking into Henry's house via the woods and dumping fertilizer in his food. He lamented taking the bag of fertilizer – saying that's what tripped him up – and wished he'd thought ahead to dish out some of the toxic chemical into a baggie. It ultimately didn't matter, though. It was over.

As for Henry's ghost, Harper spent the morning helping him cross over. He only mentioned her three boyfriends once so she put a smile on her face when dropping the dreamcatcher at his feet. He talked for another twenty minutes – mentioning different ways to shape the bushes so they didn't look uneven – before finally crossing the threshold and disappearing. Harper could only hope he found peace on the other side. For a man like Henry Spencer, that was the thing he needed most.

She planned to spend the rest of the day finishing up the Halloween decorations, but Jared surprised her by arriving early and dragging her out of the house. Luckily for her – mostly because she didn't grab a heavy coat – he didn't take her far. Instead he linked his fingers with hers, led her across the road, and then paused in front of Henry's door.

"I want to show you something," Jared answered.

"Is it in your pants?"

Jared's eyebrows flew up his forehead. "Excuse me?"

"Sorry. Zander did a trouser snake joke earlier and it stuck with me. I momentarily thought I was back in middle school. Please continue."

"I forgot what I was about to say."

"You were about to tell me what we're doing here."

"Oh, right." Jared smiled as he slipped a key into the lock and pushed open the door. "I have a little something I want to talk to you about."

"Uh-oh." Harper's heart dropped as she walked into Henry's living room. "Wow. This looks exactly like our house."

"The same company built both of them. I was struck by the similarities, too."

"Wow. I've never really looked inside. It's ... weird, huh?"

"Weird?"

"Well, it's weird to think how alike the two houses are," Harper clarified. "It's also a little sad because Henry is well and truly gone. I wonder what's going to happen to this place now. I bet Carol sells it. That's going to drive Zander nuts, especially if the neighbors aren't pre-approved and potentially boring."

"Well, funnily enough, that's kind of what I wanted to talk to you about." Jared found he was unbearably nervous as he rubbed the back of his neck. "I talked to Carol this morning and she is planning on selling the house."

"Did she say to who?"

"Actually, that's up to you and me."

"It is?" Harper was understandably confused. "She wants us to pick the people who are going to live here?"

"Wow. You're slow sometimes." Jared offered up a fluttery smile. "Let me spell it out for you. Carol is willing to sell the house to us. You and me. So wc can live here."

The admission caused Harper's stomach to do a little dance. "What?"

"You know I love you, right?"

Harper licked her lips and nodded. "I love you, too."

"The thing is, I want for us to move forward," Jared explained. "I know you do, too."

"How do you know that? I'm not saying it's not true, mind you, but I'm curious how you know that."

"Zander and I had a talk."

"I knew it! He's such a bad liar."

Jared snorted. "He may be a bad liar, but he's been surprisingly open and helpful regarding this situation. He knows that we need to come up with a way to have two households that are close to one another.

"Now, this place needs a little work, but that simply means we can afford it," he continued. "I was thinking we could both pay half the down payment and then split the mortgage payments and bills."

"And live together?"

"Yes. Does that frighten you?"

Harper immediately started shaking her head. "We're already practically living together."

"We are," Jared confirmed. "Zander is going to take over your half of the house. He will be making payments to you, though, because he only has ten grand to start with. I figure that's more than enough because it matches my ten grand for a down payment.

"Then, Shawn is moving in with Zander and he's going to pay rent directly to you until your half of the house is paid off," he continued. "We'll stay at the other house while this one is cleared out and then painted, but if all goes as planned, we should be able to get in by the end of the month."

Harper was flabbergasted. "You've really given this some thought."

"I love you and want to live with you. This is honestly the best thing for all of us. We'll have our own roof, but you'll be directly across the road from Zander. You'll be able to spend as much time together as you want and I will have a place to escape."

"Wow." Harper sucked in a breath as she turned in a circle and studied the house. "We can paint and stuff, right?"

"Absolutely. I want the carpet gone, too. I was thinking hardwood floors would be nice in the living room and new carpet in the bedrooms."

"You really have given this some thought." Harper's eyes sparkled as she turned back to him. "How miserable have you been spending time at my house?"

"I'm not miserable." Jared grabbed her hand and gave it a reassuring squeeze. "I love you. I love spending time with you. I even love spending time with Zander.

"That doesn't mean I don't want to move forward and build a life for us together," he continued. "If we do it like this, we're four people building two separate lives that often overlap. I think that's the best thing for you."

His words touched her. "What's the best thing for you?"

"Being with you."

"And this will make you happy?"

"Yes, but I need to make absolutely sure it will make you happy, too," Jared replied. "This has to work for both of us. I happen to really like this solution, but if you don't, I need you to tell me the truth. We'll come up with something else. So ... think about it. I want you to take your time."

"I don't need to take my time." Harper's lips curved as she threw her arms around Jared's neck. "This is the best idea anyone has ever come up with ... ever. I mean ever!" She rained kisses across his cheek. "I can't tell you what a relief this is."

Jared returned the hug before pulling back and focusing on her. "Because you've been worried about bringing it up?"

Harper's smile slipped, but only marginally. "Zander has a big mouth."

"He does, but in this case, I'm glad he opened it. We both were worried and afraid to talk to one another about it. Zander put my mind at ease and allowed me to think about our future. Now you and I are talking about our future. That is, if you want your future to be with me."

"Is that a trick question?"

"No, but if you're not okay with this, I need you to tell me before I sign an offer sheet."

"I want this. You have no idea how much I want this."

"Good." Jared dropped a soft kiss on her lips. "I want this, too. In fact, I'm really looking forward to it."

"Me, too." Harper grabbed him by the cheeks and excitedly smacked her lips against his. "This is like the best day ever." She escaped from his arms. "We need to get Zander."

Jared stilled. "Zander? Why? I thought you were going to reward me for coming up with the best idea ever."

"Oh, I'm going to do that ... but later."

"And what are you going to do now?"

"Make Zander come over here with his paint wheel and tape measure."

"Because?"

"Because we have to plan for our future."

"This is just a way to keep Zander involved, right?"

"Sure."

Jared wanted to believe her, but he wasn't at all convinced. "I get a say in the colors, right?"

"Once Zander and I narrow it down, you can lodge a vote. With three of us, we'll have a convenient tiebreaker."

Jared rolled his eyes. "Whatever." He tapped his cheek. "Plant another one on me. I'm going to go and watch the game with Shawn while you and Zander do whatever it is you're about to do."

Harper kissed him ... and then squealed as she stomped her feet. "This is the best day ever."

"No, it's merely the first day of the rest of our lives. We're going to have a lot of good days."

"I totally believe that."

"Good. So do I."

Made in the USA
Lexington, KY
16 October 2017